The Dream Fighter Chronicles
Book One:

Discovery!

Dear Reader:

These scrolls have come a great distance to reach your hands. Toryn, the Traveler of Worlds, brings them to you in the hopes you can read them in time. On these pages is the story of five children, not unlike you, who were asked to save the world.

Read on, but remember, these scrolls must be kept secret. All who read these pages have been carefully selected. Perhaps, one day, you will be called upon to become a Dream Fighter yourself.

Calvin Locke
Dream Fighter Transcriber

The Dream Fighter Chronicles Book One:
Discovery!
A Dream Worlds Book / October 2009

ISBN: 9780974992617

10 9 8 7 6 5 4 3 2 1

-

*To Christian —
Hope you like the
Dream World!*

Calvin Coker!

This book is dedicated to the memory of Daniel Stanley. You were only with us for such a short time, but the mark you left will stay with us forever.

Chapter One

Everything is quiet now. No one ever thought it would ever be that way, not after it all started. After everything that happened, so many crazy and unbelievable things the Dream Fighters saw, they thought they would be lucky to even breathe. We all know the world can be crazy sometimes but this is the kind of crazy you could never even think of. That's been said before, but this time, it is for real.

We owe it all to five kids. They didn't want to be heroes; they even tried not to be. We couldn't let that happen. We had to push and push them until they realized how important they were. The world was in danger and they were the only ones who had the powers to save it. They did it by finding out who they were and, most importantly, by trusting each other. You could say it was magic.

This story was not supposed to be told. It is supposed to be a secret, to protect the kids and keep the world safe. Still, the story should be told, and if you promise right now not to tell anyone about what you will soon read, then you will read a story unlike any one you've ever heard before.

It's a story of heroes, alien invaders, and the power we all have inside us that can save us. It's the story of hopes and dreams and how we can use them every day to make our lives better. Promise not to give away the secret and read on. You won't regret it.

It all started at a house on Long Island. There was a big family gathering on a Sunday, a birthday celebration. All the adults were upstairs talking about whatever adults talk about. This time, they might have been talking about the family golf trip, where all the men went to Pennsylvania to play golf while the women planned a trip somewhere else. Usually, the kids didn't have much to say about it, and this time was the same.

Jack and Braden were busy playing a game on television, *Sly Cooper*. Jack had the controller in his hands, pressing the buttons as fast as he could. Jack was eight years old, with blonde hair. He was pretty good at the game, but at this moment, he was having trouble getting past one of the monsters. He tried to jump left and got hit by the monster hard. Braden stood up quick from the couch.

"I know how to beat that monster. I did it last week. Let me show you," he said, reaching for the controller.

Jack pulled it away. "No. It's my turn. I'll get it."

"But you're doing it *wrong*," Braden insisted.

"I got it."

"No, you don't. You're gonna get killed again."

This time, Braden was right. Jack tried to jump left again and the same thing happened. He wanted to throw the controller on the floor but he had gotten in trouble two weeks ago for the same thing. Throwing controllers wasn't a nice thing to do.

Instead, he handed the controller to Braden. "Okay, it's your turn."

"It's about time." Braden took the controller. He was almost eight himself, but unlike Jack, he had dark brown hair. He was wearing a camouflage flannel shirt and tan pants, one of his favorite outfits.

He went toward the monster. It came at him with a big hammer and swung hard. Braden jumped right and avoided the swing but didn't see the next one coming. The monster clonked him on the head and he was out. He was pretty sure he knew how to beat it, but the monster was so strong. There had to be a way. If he could only remember what he did last week to get past him.

Haley was busy playing with Jillian and Gabriella, her two younger cousins. Gabriella, who was only two years old, was playing with blocks and Jillian, who was five, was helping. Haley wanted to play something else but she knew Gabby couldn't play along so she decided the right thing to do was let her play. After all, she was being quiet, which was what the adults wanted.

What Haley really wanted to do was talk about the dream she had the night before. It was really weird. She felt like she was being pulled into this circle. She wasn't scared because it wasn't scary, and in the dream she felt stronger than she ever had before. She felt like she could leap high into the air easily. She just wanted someone to explain it. The problem was, before she woke up, she heard a voice tell her not to tell anyone about it. The voice sounded familiar, like someone she knew, but she couldn't remember who. She wondered if maybe one of her cousins had ever had a dream like that. She wanted to ask really badly but she figured the best thing to do was listen to the voice. Plus, her cousins were younger than her. She was almost eleven. They wouldn't understand.

She figured everyone would just think she was crazy anyway.

"You got killed again," Jack said to Braden. "We'll never get past this monster."

"I know one way we can," Braden said, smiling.

Together, they yelled, "Uncle Johnny!"

Haley and Jack's mom came to the top of the stairs. "What do you guys want?"

"We need Uncle Johnny," Jack said.

"He's eating."

"Oh," Jack and Braden said at the top of their lungs.

"Do you want me to come down there and turn that system off?" Haley and Jack's mom, Aunt Tina, asked.

Braden and Jillian's mom came to the stairs too. "What are you doing, Braden?"

"We were trying to beat this monster and couldn't so we wanted Uncle Johnny to come downstairs and show us how," Braden said, as nicely as he could.

"Didn't Aunt Tina say he was eating?"

"Yes. But I thought everyone finished eating already."

"Uncle Johnny got here late."

"But—"

"Stop it or both Aunt Tina and I will come down there and turn the television off, do you want that?" Aunt Lisa asked.

"Well—"

"I didn't think so."

"But—"

"But nothing," Aunt Tina said. "I'll ask Uncle Johnny to come down, when he is finished eating." The last few words were said sort of angry, Haley noticed. Not *angry* angry, like when someone broke something or lied, just angry, like if Braden and Jack didn't give in, *angry* angry was coming soon.

"Okay," Jack said, and plopped down on the couch. Haley thought he was going to say something else back, but she was happy to see he was smart enough not to. Braden went back to playing the game. Jack was pretty smart, but sometimes he didn't act that way and they got yelled at for something she didn't even have anything to do with.

When Aunt Lisa and Aunt Tina were gone, Jack said, "Parents can be a pain." Haley knew he said this as a joke but he still shouldn't have said it. Sure, there were times when she got angry at her Mom and Dad, but not too many times. She was going to say something to Jack, tell him to take it back but she didn't. He probably wouldn't listen anyway.

"Oh no," Jillian said.

"What?" Haley asked.

"It's my doll. She went wee-wee again."

Jack stuck his head out from the side of the couch. "Your doll did what?"

"She went wee-wee. I gave her too much water again. When she has too much water, she goes wee-wee a lot. Now I have to change her diaper. A mommy's work is never done."

"What kind of doll goes wee-wee?"

"Baby-Wets-A-Lot," Jillian said. "I brought her and three other dolls with me today. Baby-Wets-A-Lot drinks water and then either goes wee-wee or cries. Sometimes she does both."

"That's stupid," Jack said.

"Don't be mean," Haley said.

"It's okay, Haley. Jack, you go wee-wee and cry and I bet when you were a baby you did both at the same time."

Everyone laughed, except for Jack of course. Jillian was right, everyone did that so there was a perfect reason why someone would make a doll that did. Haley wasn't so sure she would want a doll like that. Well, she had other things she wanted. One of the most important was a laptop. That would be cool, to have a laptop, so she could play games and go on websites almost anywhere. She didn't think she had much of a chance of getting one, but that wasn't going to stop her from asking, that's for sure.

Braden and Jack tried to beat that level of the game a few times more but they got bored because they just couldn't get past that one part. Haley was tempted to try herself but she didn't think she'd have a chance and she didn't want to fight to get a turn.

Just when it seemed like Jack and Braden were about to give up, Uncle Johnny came down the stairs.

"I hear someone's having trouble down here," Uncle Johnny said.

"We can't get past this monster," Braden said, "We tried going left and right but he keeps getting us."

"I even tried jumping," Jack said, "just like you showed us but it doesn't work. Maybe the controller is broken."

"We haven't been *throwing* the controller, have we?"

"No," Jack said. "I thought about it but remembered I am not supposed to do it, so I didn't."

"Good. Now, what part are you stuck on?"

Jack and Braden showed the part they couldn't beat and Uncle Johnny remembered it was the same part they had a problem with the week before. It was pretty tough, but Uncle Johnny knew the trick and showed it to them again.

"You have to jump and swing at the same time. That throws the monster off balance so you can sneak past him on the right. Sometimes you don't have to knock out the monsters to beat them. Sometimes you have to use your smarts and beat them that way."

"You don't have to beat them up?" Braden asked.

"Not all the time. A lot of these monsters are bigger than your character. Your character is smarter than them, and so are you. So use that."

"I like beating them up," Jack said.

"So do I," Braden agreed.

Uncle Johnny turned and looked at Haley. "Silly boys."

"You got that right. I am the one who has to be around them all the time."

"Maybe you should show them how silly they are sometimes."

"Good idea."

"Okay guys, I got you past this part. Think you can take it from here?" Uncle Johnny asked.

"Sure," Braden said, "it's my turn so I can take it."

"No, it's my turn," Jack said, trying to take the controller from Braden, "you remember, you died last."

"But I still had one more life left," Braden insisted.

"No, no. You got killed twice. Every two lives we change turns."

"Enough," Uncle Johnny said. "I don't care whose turn it was. If you guys don't stop, I'll keep playing, and you know it will be a long time before I die."

"Oh," Braden and Jack said.

"Do you guys want to keep playing?"

"Yes."

"Then learn to get along. I could tell you who goes next but I want you to solve this yourself. You guys are cousins, right?"

"Yeah," they answered.

"And friends?"

"Yes, but—"

"Hey, what's rule number one?" Uncle Johnny asked.

Haley smiled, rolled her eyes, and said along with Jack, "Listen to Uncle Johnny."

"And rule number two?"

"Listen to Uncle Johnny."

"Okay, then. So, like I was saying. You are cousins and friends. You shouldn't fight, you should be nice to each other. You guys figure this out. I am coming back down here in a minute and I want to see you guys getting along, not fighting over something silly like whose turn it is. There are more important things than that."

Haley agreed. Getting a laptop was certainly more important than arguing over who got to play some stupid game first. But, like Uncle Johnny said, silly boys. Haley wondered how silly Uncle Johnny was when he was a boy. Probably pretty silly, she thought.

Chapter Two

After they sang 'Happy Birthday' the kids came back downstairs and the boys went back to playing their game. The boys started to play the way Uncle Johnny taught them, but before long they were trying to beat up the monsters instead of sneaking around them. Haley watched for a little while, and every time they tried to attack the monster, she could see a way to sneak around it. She tried to tell them, but it seemed like they had their 'Girl Ear Filters' on, as they had called them once, and couldn't hear her.

Haley was tired, and felt even more so when she saw both Gabby and Jillian sleeping on the couch. She sat next to them, telling herself that she wouldn't go to sleep, just rest her eyes a bit. Jack and Braden, frustrated with the game, sat on the couch across from her. It looked like they were going to go to sleep, too. She closed her eyes, and felt the darkness wrap around her like when she went to bed. She fought to stay awake.

Luckily, her brother and cousin helped out.

"Uncle Johnny!" they yelled and yelled, trying to get him to come downstairs to help them with the game again.

Haley opened her eyes and rubbed them. They felt itchy like when she woke up in the morning, but she hadn't even been sitting down for four minutes. She could see the clock on the cable box, so she knew she wasn't crazy.

"Can anyone hear us?" Braden asked. "We're having trouble with the game again."

Braden had said that pretty loud, but no one answered. That wasn't normal. It didn't take much noise for *someone* to come downstairs. Braden yelled again, and Jack joined him.

Nothing happened.

Haley started to worry, but she didn't want to let the rest of them know it. She was the oldest and she had to keep her cool, even if inside, she felt anything but. She tried to think what could possibly be happening, then remembered that Uncle Michael had brought over a video and the adults were probably upstairs watching it in the kitchen and couldn't hear them.

Still, the TV in the kitchen had to be pretty loud, and she didn't hear anything coming from upstairs at all.

"Where is he?" Jack asked.

"I don't know. Maybe they are busy upstairs," Haley answered, trying to sound like she believed what she said, even when she didn't. She figured that was probably what her parents did a lot.

"He must be sleeping," Braden said.

"But Uncle Johnny only falls asleep on Christmas Eve," Jack said, "he never does it any other time."

"He could be tired," Braden said.

Jillian sat up. "What's going on?"

"We can't get Uncle Johnny to come downstairs. No one is answering," Braden answered.

"Is *that* all? I can get him to come down here."

Jillian jumped off the couch and ran up the stairs. She stopped at the top of them, like she ran into a wall. Her head hurt a little, but that didn't make sense. She could see the hallway, but couldn't go past the top of the stairs.

"Ouch," she said, rubbing her forehead.

"What?" Haley asked.

"Something's in my way."

"Huh?"

"Yeah, I can't get past the stairs," Jillian said.

"Is the dog gate in the way?"

"I would have seen *that.*"

"Okay."

Haley ran toward Jillian, and she got there quicker than she would have expected to. She didn't really notice it until Jack said something.

"Wow," he said. Jack said 'wow' a lot, but this one sounded serious.

"Wow what?" Haley asked.

"You just ran through the air," he said.

"Through the air?"

"Yeah, almost like you were floating."

Haley had sort of felt that, but she didn't think it was anything. "So?"

"So, it was cool. Can you do it again?"

"Um, no. I have to see what Jillian is talking about." Haley made it to the top of the stairs and put her hand out toward the hallway. Before she could get her hand past the top step, she felt something push her back. It wasn't hard, like an invisible wall. It was more like trying to stretch a rubber band further than it is supposed to go, only this didn't snap.

"That's weird," she said, looking at Jillian. Jillian just shrugged her shoulders.

"I can't get upstairs."

"We better call someone," Haley said.

With that, everyone starting yelling for their mommies and daddies, and no one answered. Gabby had woken up from all the noise. She looked at everyone. Jack was the closest to her, and when he looked at her, he felt like he couldn't look away. It was like Gabby had control of his eyes and wouldn't let go.

"Gabby, stop it," he said, but she just smiled at him. Jack felt the urge to get something for her, but he didn't know what she wanted.

Haley looked at Jillian and said, "We have to do something."

Jillian seemed like she was ready to cry but she held herself together as best she could. Haley put her hand on her shoulder. Normally, Haley would want to cry too, but for some reason she felt a calm feeling come over her, telling her she had to take control and everything would be okay.

"We just have to think, Jilly. Think."

"Okay."

Jillian closed her eyes and squeezed them shut, like she was really thinking hard. Haley thought she looked funny doing that, but she closed her eyes and did the same thing, so if Jillian opened her eyes for a second, she wouldn't feel bad.

Jack still felt trapped by Gabby, not in a bad way, but he couldn't look away. He could tell now that Gabby wanted a doll. But it wasn't just any doll, it was a particular doll, a doll he had seen before. A picture came to his mind.

Then, he knew what she wanted: Baby-Wets-A-Lot.

He looked around and couldn't find the doll, but he felt like he really needed to. He looked on both couches, under the old wooden table in the center of the room. He found a football they had been looking for, a couple of Lego's, an empty Capri-Sun, but no doll.

"Just try to think of something that can get us out of this," Haley said to Jillian, both of their eyes still closed tightly shut.

Braden had been quiet through all of this because he had noticed something but didn't know how to tell everyone else. When he had looked at the Playstation controller, he was pretty sure he made it move. He couldn't be completely sure, but he was as sure as he had ever been about something. He wanted to try it again, but he was scared. No one could move things by just thinking about doing it. That was stuff you saw in the movies, not something you could do in real life. At least, that was what his parents and other adults had told him.

He stared at the controller, but it didn't move. Maybe he had just thought he had moved the controller the first time. There was no way to know. Maybe he had to do something special to make it work. He really had no idea and there was no way to know for sure.

"Hey, did anyone see Baby-Wets-A-Lot? Gabby wants it" Jack asked. He wondered if anyone would ask how he knew that. He hoped they didn't.

Jillian and Haley didn't answer. Jack could see they had their eyes closed like they were thinking about something. Jack felt another nudge in his mind from Gabby. It seemed like she was getting impatient and really wanted Jillian's doll, the one that went wee-wee all the time.

"I see it," Braden said. He pointed to a spot next to the TV, and Jack walked over to grab it. Before he got halfway there, the doll lifted off the ground and floated over toward Gabby.

"What the--?" Jack asked.

The doll kept floating across the room and landed softly on Gabby's lap, like it was following Braden's finger.

"I did that!" Braden said.

"How?" Jack asked.

"How should I know? I just did it, that's all I know. I did it before with the game controller."

"When?"

"A minute ago."

"I didn't see that," Jack said.

"You don't believe me?"

"I just said I didn't see it."

"But you just saw me do that with the doll, right?" Braden asked.

"Well, I saw the doll float across the room."

"Yes. I did that!"

Haley opened her eyes. "What are you guys talking about? We are trying to think of a plan here."

"Braden said he made Jillian's doll fly and that he made the Playstation controller move without his hands."

"What?"

"I did it, I swear!" Braden insisted.

"Come on, there's no way you did that. That's like, magic or something," Jack said.

"I did it."

"No way."

"Yes way."

"Guys, guys, you gotta stop arguing if you have any chance of getting out of here," a familiar voice said.

"Who said that?" Braden asked.

"Doll talk," Gabby said, smiling.

"What?" Haley asked.

"Doll talk. Doll talk," Gabby said again.

"Doll talk?" the familiar voice said, and it sounded like it was coming from Gabby.

"Uh-oh," Jillian said. She had an idea why the doll was talking.

"Uh-oh what?" Haley asked, looking back at Jillian, who opened her eyes.

"I think I did that," Jillian answered.

"Did what, made that voice?"

"No."

"Then what?"

"Yeah, what's with this 'Doll talk' stuff," the male voice said.

"Doll talk," Gabby said, laughing. "Uncle." It sounded like she said a name after uncle, but no one understood what she said.

"You told me to think of something, Haley, so I did."

"What did you think of?"

"Well, I thought of my Mommy and Daddy first, but not too much. Then I thought about something Uncle Johnny said today, and it made me laugh. Then I heard Jack talk about my doll."

"Um, okay," Haley said.

"Oh boy," Uncle Johnny's voice said.

Chapter Three

Everyone turned to look at Baby-Wets-A-Lot. That was certainly where the voice came from. The doll looked the same, sitting on Gabby's lap. Haley looked close, to see if it was moving. At first, it wasn't. Then, the doll moved its eyes.

"Jilly, does Baby-Wets-A-Lot move her eyes?" she asked. She had seen dolls do that before.

Jillian was still at the top of the stairs. "No. She just cries."

"I'm a doll?" Uncle Johnny asked.

Everyone jumped from surprise. The doll was talking and moving its mouth. Now they knew for sure something crazy was going on. First Haley leaped, then Braden was moving things with his mind. Now, their Uncle was speaking through a doll.

"First the doll flies, and now it talks?" Jack asked.

"It didn't fly. I made it fly," Braden reminded him.

"Right. Either way, this is weird."

"Not as weird as me being stuck in a doll," Uncle Johnny said. "But, I am a cool doll, right? G.I. Joe, or like an action figure or something?"

"Um, you're a Ba—"

Haley covered Braden's mouth. "You're an okay doll, Uncle Johnny. It's a baby, but it's normal looking."

"Yeah, and when you drink water you—"

"Aren't thirsty any more," Haley interrupted. "You're just a normal doll."

"A baby? I am a baby? All these years I spent growing up, working hard and now I am stuck as a baby?" Tears started to fall from the doll's face. "A baby?" Uncle

Johnny cried uncontrollably. It was what Baby-Wets-A-Lot did.

"It's okay."

"I'm, I'm, crying?"

"Yes, the doll you are in can cry and do a whole lot of other cool things."

"I'm a girly doll, aren't I?" Uncle Johnny said through tears. "A silly, girly doll."

"Baby-Wets-A-Lot is not a silly doll," Jillian said.

"What? Baby who?"

"Baby-Works-A lot," Haley said. "You're a doll that helps Mommy work around the house."

"Then why am I in a dress?"

"Jillian put that on the doll. We can change it if you want."

"Yeah, I think I'd like that. Being a baby is one thing, but having to wear a dress, that's just too much. Know what I mean?" The tears stopped a little. It seemed Uncle Johnny was getting a hold of himself again.

"I think so. Do you know what's happening?"

"Of course I do."

"What?" Jack asked.

"Yeah, tell us," Braden said.

"Where is everyone?" Jillian asked, finally coming down the stairs.

"Well, it's kind of complicated, where everyone is. I'd first have to tell you where you are."

"Where did you come from?" Jack asked. "Was everyone else there with you?"

"I really don't know. I was sleeping when Jillian called for me and brought me here."

"How did she do that?" Braden asked.

"Yeah, how did I do that? I know that I thought of you, but how did I bring you here?"

"It's your Dream Power. If you think of something you can make it appear."

"So, I can make my Mommy and Daddy appear right now too?"

"Sorry, that you can't do. You can only call on one person to help you, and you called me. Good thing, though, because I was the one who was supposed to help you."

"Did you say that was her Dream Power?" Braden asked. "Like we are in a dream right now?"

"Well, sort of a dream and sort of not. This isn't the *real* real world, but things that happen here are just as important. Think of it like another world."

"Like an alternate reality?" Jack asked, "I saw that on a cartoon. I think it was *Jimmy Neutron.*"

"Exactly like that. That's why you feel like you are awake. But in this world, you can do things that you couldn't do in the other one. Everyone has a Dream Power. You all have more than one. There are all sorts of powers. For example, someone who can't walk in the other world can in this one."

"Everyone has them?" Jillian asked.

"Yup. Most people don't even notice because they don't think this world is real at all. They think it is just dreaming but it is much more than that."

"But this *is* a dream," Haley said.

"Like I said, sort of. Sort of like the dream you had the other night."

Haley looked the other way. "What dream?"

"You know, the one I told you not to tell anyone about. The one where you felt like you were being pulled into something. That something was this world. I was trying to show you but you weren't ready."

"That was you?"

"Of course it was. Didn't you recognize my voice?"

"Not really. It sounded familiar, but I wasn't sure. Who was the boy with the long blonde hair?"

"We'll talk about him at another time. What's important now is that you guys identify your Dream Powers and learn how to use them."

"What's your Dream Power?" Jack asked.

"I have many powers because I have been training for a long time. Right now, I don't think I have any real powers because I am in this doll. But, you did say this is a cool doll, so I am sure I will be able to do something."

Jack and Braden laughed and Haley kicked Jack in the leg to get him to stop. The kick hurt and Jack said so, but Haley didn't even look at him. He should have known that Uncle Johnny wouldn't want to know that he was stuck in a baby that went wee-wee.

"You probably will find out soon," Haley said. She actually had to hold back from laughing herself. It was pretty funny.

"Have you guys noticed anything strange other than what Jillian can do?"

"I can move things with my mind," Braden said.

"That's called Telekinesis, and it is a very special power. You have to be careful with it. You can't just move anything, or everything would be going in different directions. You have to concentrate, and you have to relax. Most important, and this goes for all of your powers, you can't doubt yourself. You have to believe you can do the things you do or they won't work at all."

"Okay," all the kids answered. They really weren't sure what to think of all of this, but they were pretty sure Uncle Johnny wouldn't lie to them. They needed to trust someone right then. They were all a little scared, and Uncle Johnny was the only adult around. Maybe he could help them find their parents.

"With that power, Braden, you can move objects big and small. Don't worry about the size. But there are a few other rules."

"Rules?" Braden asked. Every time something cool came along, there were always rules. If this power was like anything else, Uncle Johnny was going to tell him he had to share it.

"Yes, rules. Like, rule number one, you can't doubt yourself. That goes for all of you." The doll moved its head a little and Gabby got scared. She knocked it off her, sending it toward the floor. Haley raced over in one leap and grabbed it before it landed.

"Thanks," Uncle Johnny said. He turned his head and looked over at Gabby. "Sorry. I didn't mean to scare you." Gabby just laughed.

"You were saying about rules," Braden said, and it was obvious he didn't like the word 'rules'. What kid does?

"Yes. For your power, you have two other rules. One is that you can't move a living thing. Anything that has its own mind cannot be moved through telekinesis. Got it?"

"Like animals?"

"Yes," Uncle Johnny said.

"What about trees? They don't have a mind, do they?"

"Yes, they kind of do, Braden. A tree can search for water with its roots in the toughest places. It can sense water. They can break through big metal pipes just to get to the water in them. They also can lean one direction or another to get more light. Also, if a tree is sick, you can rip off part of its bark and it will fight to live."

"They didn't teach us that in school," Jack said.

"No, they haven't gotten to that stuff yet I guess. I have a feeling you are going to learn a lot of things today that you were never taught and probably never will be taught in school."

"Right, like telekinesis," Braden said.

"Exactly. Your second rule, for now at least, is that you can only move things for a short period of time. After that you'll get really tired, so don't push it, okay?"

"Got it."

"What about Haley?" Jack asked. "She moved before like a superhero or something."

"I saw that when she caught me. Haley, you have the ability to soar through the air. It's not super speed, like someone else here has, but instead, you can make yourself light and jump really high."

"Very cool," Haley said, "but how do I control it?"

"You really don't have to. You just have to believe, and you can jump to the top of a house if you want to," Uncle Johnny said. Jack felt funny talking to a doll, and he figured everyone else did too. Every time Uncle Johnny spoke, Jack wanted to laugh.

"That's it? No other rules?"

"Well, you can't jump *too* high into the air because you can hurt yourself when you come back down. You'll have to test it out and see what the limits are. Also, like Braden, you can't use your power too much or it will tire you out, especially if you are new at it."

"Okay, that seems easy enough."

"What about me?" Jack asked.

"Well, you were the one I was talking about when I mentioned super speed. You can run faster than any car, and with training, even faster than that. You can go long distances in seconds. And, even though your power really doesn't have any rules, there are a few things you should know."

"Like what?" Jack asked. He had a really big grin on his face, Haley noticed, like when he knew they were going to get pizza. Pizza was Jack's favorite food.

"Well, if you can go that fast, you have to be careful not to run into anything, right?"

"I guess so."

"Also, you have to be careful not to get lost."

"Okay," Jack said, already sounding a little impatient, like he wanted to start running right then. Haley wondered, with the stairs blocked, where he thought he was going to run to.

"And if you stop focusing on running, you'll slow down. If you get scared, you'll speed up, but that's dangerous. So pay attention, okay?"

"Yeah, no problem Uncle Johnny. I can do all that."

"Good."

"Uncle Johnny?" Haley asked.

"Yes Haley?"

"What about Gabby, does she have any powers?"

"Of course she does. Jack knows what it is."

"I do?"

"Yeah. I noticed it before. She made you do something for her, didn't you?"

"Uh-huh. She made me get the Baby-We--, um, the doll for her," Jack said, remembering Haley kicked him the last time he almost said something about the doll.

"She's got the charm power. If you look into her eyes, she can make you do whatever she wants. Be careful, because she is little, and she doesn't have much control over it. Try not to look directly into her eyes. And if she gets angry, she can drive you nuts, if you know what I mean."

"Gabby never gets angry," Jillian said.

"I am sure she does sometimes," Uncle Johnny answered, "but that's not important. You all know what your powers are and you are going to need them. Also, you all are stronger in this world than you are in the other one. Again, you are going to need that for what's coming."

"What's coming?" Braden asked as he floated the television remote in the air. He seemed to have good control over his power already. Jack wanted to see how his worked but he couldn't do it in the small basement. He'd end up running into one of the walls.

"I can't say I know for sure. I just know there is trouble, and we have been expecting it for a while now. We used to have other Dream Fighters to handle this, but we haven't trained a lot lately and we need new recruits. It's kind of hard to explain it all to you."

"Dream Fighters?"

"Yeah, that's what we call you guys. How do you like the name?"

"I think it is kind of cool," Braden said.

"Me too," added Jillian.

"Good, cause it's not like they are going to change it or something. Anyway, we needed to get some other young people involved because our last team has gotten to the point where it is time for them to retire. When they get older, they stop believing and are not as powerful as they should be."

"I thought you got stronger when you got older," Jack said.

"Yes, you can lift heavier things, and maybe run faster and hit a golf ball farther, but your belief gets weaker. You forget to believe actually. It's sad, but it kind of happens to everyone."

"Even you?" Jillian asked.

Uncle Johnny laughed. It seemed odd coming from a doll. "Even me, though a lot of people say I don't act as old as I am. In this case, that's a good thing."

"So, what's coming?" Jack asked. "You said we needed these powers because something is coming."

"We think it is Sarlak."

"Who?" Braden asked. "Who's Sarlak?"

"He's is leading a group from the planet called Gorgon. We are not really sure who he is, but the Gorgons are a race of people seven feet tall. They have been convinced by Sarlak to attack us. We don't know why. We just know we have to stop them. They are messy, ugly, and they have really bad breath."

Everyone laughed.

"It's not funny. Their breath is bad. Trust me; you don't want to be stuck in an elevator full of Gorgons. You'll pass out."

"Well, I won't need to use an elevator any more. I'll just jump to the floor I want to go to," Haley said.

"And I can run up the stairs," Jack added.

"If there's something upstairs I need, I'll just think about it," Jillian said.

"And I can use my mind to bring it to me," said Braden.

"Right, and Gabby will just get one of you guys to do it for you. Still, I'm sorry that your first assignment is with these creatures. It won't be very easy. The good thing is although they are very strong, they are also not so bright. We should be able to outsmart them."

"What do we have to do, kill them?" Braden asked.

"No, probably not. We're going to try and avoid fighting them."

"And we have to do it?"

"Yes. They have decided to bring their army here. That's why we brought you into this world, to bring them here. Hopefully we can stop them from launching an attack on Earth."

"But I thought this wasn't Earth."

"Well, it is. And things that happen here have an effect on what you call the real world. I left a trap for the Gorgons. They should be coming here soon. So, practice your skills. Jack, you'll have to wait, it's too dangerous for you to practice running down here. All I want you to do is think about how fast you can run. Just keep picturing it in your mind, okay?"

"Okay."

"The rest of you, start training. We got a big day ahead of us."

Chapter Four

So, they practiced their powers. Haley worked on floating, something Uncle Johnny told her how to do. It was hard for him to do that being stuck in a doll, but Haley got the hang of it. After a few minutes, she started to get tired, and he told her to stop, because they had work to do and she needed her energy.

Jillian had found a pair of doll jeans and a shirt that fit Uncle Johnny, so he would stop complaining about having to wear a dress. She didn't see why it was such a big deal, but it was kind of her fault that he was stuck in Baby-Wets-A-Lot in the first place.

"Now, that's better," Uncle Johnny said. "Wait, am I wearing a diaper?"

"Yes," Jillian said.

"Okay, simple question here. Why?"

"It came with the doll," Haley said, floating over to where they were.

"You can't take it off?"

"It wouldn't be a good idea. It would ruin the doll."

"Ruin the doll?" Uncle Johnny asked.

"Yes, it's attached. Plus, you never know when you might need it," Haley said, hoping that would end the talk about it.

"All right." Uncle Johnny turned his head toward Jillian. "Next time, could you pick something different?"

"I'm sorry," Jillian answered.

"It's okay. I'd prefer something a little more, um, manly, next time, if you know what I mean. G.I. Joe, maybe. Something like that."

"Okay Uncle Johnny."

Jillian had practiced thinking of things and making them appear but she kept losing focus and getting things that weren't exactly what she wanted. She tried to think of a cup she liked but instead she got a different one. It was still a cup, but not the one she wanted. Uncle Johnny said this was normal, that Jillian's power was the most difficult and needed the most concentration. As she practiced more and more, she got better, almost to the point where she didn't call something she didn't want. It was tough.

Braden was having a pretty easy time controlling things. He could float two objects at one time. He even was able to prevent himself from getting weak when he did it. He was ready to try three, but Uncle Johnny told him to wait for that. Most times, one was more than enough. To be able to float two was excellent.

What was more important was that Braden learn not only how to float things, but to send them at something. It was tough to practice in the basement, but Uncle Johnny said Braden needed to be able to sling things at the enemy when the time came for that.

"Sling them?" Braden asked.

"Yes, like if you could take a rock and send it at someone trying to attack you so you can get away."

"Oh, I get it. I did something like that in a video game one time."

"Yes, exactly like that." Uncle Johnny looked at Haley. "Pick me up."

Haley walked over and picked him up. "Where do you want to go?" she asked.

"Over there," Uncle Johnny pointed, to a spot by the stairs. "I am pretty sure I saw a Nerf ball over there before."

"I know the one you are talking about, the blue football," Jack said.

"That's it."

"We took it outside before," Jack said.

"Well, that won't work. We're not ready to go upstairs yet."

After a moment, Uncle Johnny had an idea. "Jillian?"

"Yes Uncle Johnny?"

"Do you know the ball I am talking about?"

"I think so. The blue one Jack and Braden were throwing in the backyard?" she asked.

"That's it. Can you get it for me?"

"I'll try."

"No, Jillian. Don't try. Do it. Believe."

Jillian crinkled her nose at Uncle Johnny and then closed her eyes. Again, it looked like she was thinking really hard. Everyone watched her and waited for something to happen. For almost a minute, nothing did.

Then, seemingly out of nowhere, a blue Nerf football fell to the ground by Jillian's feet.

"Wow," Braden said, "that was good."

"Okay Braden. Now I want you to practice slinging that ball into the wall over there. I wanted the Nerf ball so you don't hurt anyone or break anything."

"No problem." Braden floated the ball close to him then slung it against the wall. The ball traveled fast and it made a loud 'thud'.

"That's good," Uncle Johnny said, "but try to do it harder. Make it like a missile."

"But aren't Nanny and Pop gonna be mad at me if I break something on the wall?"

"No, this isn't really Nanny and Pop's house," Jillian said.

"Well, it is and it isn't," Uncle Johnny answered. "Still, you don't want to go and break something in any house. No one would like that very much."

Braden nodded and went back to practicing.

"Okay, we need to get some stuff together. First, we need some food."

"Yeah, I'm hungry," Jack said.

"You're always hungry," Haley said.

"There's nothing wrong with that. That's how you get bigger and stronger, by eating," Uncle Johnny said.

"Until you become a doll," Braden said, not taking his eyes off the football.

"You just worry about practicing, wise guy. For the rest of you, it's time to get the supplies together. Go into the pantry in the laundry room and grab some stuff to eat. I am sure Nanny has a whole load of food. And don't go grabbing all junk. Get something that is good for you."

"We know," Jack said. He walked into the laundry room and turned on the light. "How are Lunchables?"

"Fine with me. I won't be eating them. I *am* thirsty, though."

"I'm not so sure that the doll can drink anything," Haley said.

"Sure she, um, he can," Jillian said excitedly. "It's one of the things the doll can do."

Haley looked at Jillian with a stern face. "But now is not the time for Uncle Johnny to be finding out what the doll can and can't do, right?"

It took a second, but Jillian got it. "Oh, right."

"Is there something you guys want to tell me?" Uncle Johnny asked, sounding a little worried.

"Nope. Everything's good. Don't worry," Haley answered. She knew it wouldn't be long before Uncle Johnny figured it out but she wanted to take as much time as possible. She was pretty sure he wasn't going to like it.

"Why do I feel like I *should* worry?" Uncle Johnny asked.

"Probably because you are stuck in the body of a doll and don't feel like yourself," Haley said. She was proud of herself for being able to convince Uncle Johnny that everything would be okay even when she knew he would most likely be going wee-wee soon.

"Well, I guess that makes sense."

"Trust me," Haley said.

"I found a box of Capri-Suns," Jack yelled from the pantry.

"What flavor?" Uncle Johnny asked.

'Tropical Punch."

"That sounds fine. Bring the box. And try to find a backpack. I think I saw one in the laundry room."

"You mean something like this?" Jillian asked, holding up a pink Dora the Explorer backpack.

"Good job. Not my first choice on color, but you did fine."

Jack came out with the box of drinks and what looked to be about eight Lunchables. "This good?"

"It should be fine," Uncle Johnny said. "Now throw as much of it as you can into the backpack. It shouldn't be too heavy."

Jack did as Uncle Johnny asked, and without being told, Braden helped. When they were done, they carried the backpack over to Uncle Johnny.

"How heavy is it?"

Jack lifted it up pretty easily. "Not too bad."

"Remember, someone is going to have to carry that on their back for a while. You guys are stronger here, but that strength doesn't last forever. You can get tired."

Haley walked over and put it on her back. "I could carry this. It's about as heavy as my backpack for my school books is. It should be fine for me," she said.

"Okay then. Now, I want you to continue practicing for a little bit longer. I won't be able to talk to you for what will feel like half an hour, so be sure to behave. Don't worry, I will be back."

"But Uncle Johnny, don't leave," Jillian said, "We're scared."

"Remember rule number one?"

Haley and Jack said, "Listen to Uncle—"

Uncle Johnny laughed. "No, not *that* rule number one. The other one."

"Don't doubt ourselves?" Braden asked.

"That's it. Don't. And believe in each other, too. It's sort of the same thing and it will definitely help you. And, I will be back very soon. I promise."

Then, the doll went back to looking the way it did before Uncle Johnny started talking through it. It went lifeless in Jillian's hands, and she almost dropped it because it shocked her for it to change so quickly.

"Okay, we should practice," Haley said. "If we keep doing that, it will make the time go by faster."

No one argued with her. Everyone, except Gabby and Jack, practiced their abilities. Jack went over to where Gabby was sitting and put her on his lap. He wanted to watch TV but didn't know if it would work and he figured someone would get mad at him for doing trying to turn it on. So he just stared at the wall and thought about what it would be like to move real fast like Uncle Johnny said he would be able to. He had seen cartoon shows where boys could do that and it was something he always wanted to be able to do. He could be a better baseball player that way. He wondered if anyone in the Major Leagues would be able to run as fast as he could.

Jack wished that his abilities in the dream world worked in the real one. He would be able to impress his friends by how fast he could run. If he got into trouble, he could just run away and no one would be able to catch him. That would be great. Of course, he figured Uncle Johnny would say it was better to not get into trouble at all.

About twenty minutes passed by, and Jillian came over and sat on the couch. She looked tired.

"I miss Uncle Johnny," she said. "I keep trying to wish him back here but he's not coming."

"He said he would be here in half an hour," Haley said.

"Isn't it half an hour already?"

"No," Jack answered.

"How long is half an hour?" Jillian asked.

Haley thought for a bit. *She* knew how long half an hour was, but it was hard to explain it to someone who didn't. Then, she had an idea.

"Do you know how long a TV show lasts?"

"I think so."

"Well, it's about that long. Most TV shows anyway."

"That's a long time," Jillian said. "And Uncle Johnny's been gone a long time, so shouldn't he be back already?"

"He should be back in about five minutes," Braden said, "If I timed it right. My new watch has a timer on it. I set it right when Uncle Johnny said he was leaving."

"That's cool," Jack said.

"Thanks. Hey, I want something to eat."

"Uncle Johnny didn't say we should eat yet."

"He didn't say we shouldn't, either."

"Well, I don't think he wants us to," Haley said.

"I think he doesn't care," Jack said. "And I am hungry too. Let's eat."

"You can't wait less than five minutes?"

"I could go for a snack too," Jillian said, rubbing her belly. "I can't remember the last time I ate something."

"All you guys have to do is wait a couple of minutes."

"There's other stuff to eat in the laundry room. I saw Doritos and potato chips and a whole bunch of other stuff."

"Just wait," Haley said, raising her voice so they would listen to her. She figured they probably wouldn't, but she had to try.

"Nah," Braden said.

Haley floated over to the door to the laundry room. "I am not letting you in," she said.

"Who made you boss?"

"I am the oldest, so you have to listen to me."

"No we don't," Jack said.

"Maybe we should listen to her," Jillian said, making this another boys against girls fight.

"She's not my mother, and she isn't Uncle Johnny," Jack said, "I say we eat."

With that, Jack tried to run past her. It was like one big blur going toward the laundry room. Haley felt very angry that no one would listen to her. She felt something tingly on her skin. She knelt down to try and block Jack.

Then, something really strange happened. A bubble formed around her. Jack bounced into the bubble, came almost within an inch of hitting her, then bounced back, crashing onto the couch. Haley wasn't sure if he was hurt. She would have felt very bad if he was. She didn't want to hurt him.

"I want to eat now!" Braden yelled, and put his hand out like he was going to hurl something at Haley. There was nothing to throw. Instead, a small purple ball of energy came from his palm and shot at Haley.

The bubble was still around her, and the energy ball bounced off of it and into the ceiling, where it left a small burn mark.

"Uh-oh," Braden said. "I am sorry Haley. I didn't mean to do that."

"It's okay," Haley said as she watched the bubble disappear. "Just don't do it again. That would have hurt."

Haley walked over to where Jack was. He was sitting up, and rubbing his shoulder. "That hurt," he said.

"It was your fault," Haley said, even though she really wanted to say she was sorry. She was just angry at Jack for trying to run at her in the first place. "Are you okay?"

"I think so. My shoulder hurts a little."

"You're all lucky that's all that happened," Uncle Johnny said.

"You're back, thank goodness," Jillian said.

"Yes. You see what happened?"

"I just wanted to get something to eat and Haley wouldn't let me," Braden said, sounding as nice as possible.

"I am the oldest, so I thought I should be the one to tell people what to do."

"Leading has nothing to do with telling people what to do, Haley. Unless, you are sure you know what the right thing to do is. Were you sure you knew that?"

"No," Haley said, "I didn't mean to do anything wrong."

"I didn't say you did. Really, you all did something wrong. You didn't trust each other in a bad situation. You didn't listen to each other. Imagine if this was during something really important. It would have been worse. And, you guys did the worst thing you could do in this situation. You got angry without control."

"We didn't mean to," Jillian said.

"I didn't want to do what I did to Haley," Braden added. He really looked upset. He was a little scared about what happened.

"I know. You have other powers I didn't get a chance to explain. Some of them will come out when you are out of control and angry. You have to be very careful. Also, if you are scared, crazy things can happen, so try to stay calm whenever you can. You could have hurt each other."

Uncle Johnny turned the doll's head to look at Jack. "And I thought I told you not to go racing around the room, that you could get hurt if you did."

"I don't know what happened Uncle Johnny. It was like I really wanted something to eat. That I *had* to have something to eat or I would go nuts."

"Hmm," Uncle Johnny said. "Okay, that makes sense. And I think someone here really is hungry."

"I would like something," Braden said.

"No, it's not you. It's Gabby."

"How do you know?" Haley asked.

"She linked with Jack before to get her the doll. They might still have that link. When she decided she wanted something to eat, she might have just made him do what he did to get it."

"I had her on my lap," Jack said.

"That could do it. Anything could do it, really. That's why you have to be careful, and you have to make sure that what you are doing is what you want to do. Control your urges."

"Urges?" Jillian asked.

"Oh, sorry. You have to control what you want. As I am sure your mommies and daddies have told you, you can't always have what you want. And on top of that, you have to make sure it is what you want, not what someone else does."

"Oh," Jillian said.

"I'm really not that hungry at all," Jack said. "That's scary, that she can do that."

"You all have special powers, like I said. Haley, you learned how to protect yourself. And Braden, you found a new power too."

"An energy ball shot from my hand!"Braden said, excited.

"Well, that's not exactly a good thing. You used it as an anger power. You got really angry, probably just because you are trapped here, a little scared about what's going to happen, and maybe frustrated that you can't do anything about it right now. That sound like it makes sense?"

Braden nodded. "I'm really sorry."

"It's nice that you apologized, but it's okay. You really didn't mean it, and I think Haley and everyone else knows it. You don't want to hurt anyone. None of you do. Just remember that, and try to control yourselves, okay?"

"Okay," everyone answered.

"It won't be easy, but you have to remember that. And you have to decide to agree on things, especially if there is an emergency. Or if I am not around for a minute and something has to be done. You guys can choose a leader if you want, but remember, being a leader isn't about telling people what to do. You have to listen and then decide. It takes a lot of work."

The kids thought about that for a minute, and no one said they wanted to be leader. Everyone thought Uncle Johnny was going to pick Haley because she was the oldest. That was what adults usually did. When they were down in the basement, Haley was always told she was in charge.

"No, it doesn't have to be Haley," Uncle Johnny said, "I know that's what you guys are thinking."

"How did you know?" Jillian asked.

"It had to be what you guys were thinking. Haley has to want to be the leader, and you guys have to agree. It won't work any other way."

"I'll do it if everyone wants me to," Haley said, because she thought that's what she was supposed to say.

"That's not exactly the way you should volunteer. Why don't you guys think about that for a little while. Before that, I'll tell you about who you will be facing, and what you have to do."

Uncle Johnny told them the story of the Gorgons, and how their big leader, Lord D'Raygon, was the one who was causing trouble. They came from a galaxy far away from Earth, right near the North Star. They had been friendly in the past but recently became evil and angry and wanted to attack Earth.

"I thought you said the bad guy was Sarlak," Jack said.

"We thought so. It turns out that the Lord is on his way himself. This is important for them. Sarlak is the evil one, and he has taken control of the Lord's mind. You guys need to show him that he is wrong, that we were friends and they shouldn't do this," Uncle Johnny explained.

"But this isn't Earth," Braden said.

"It isn't. But if this world, the dream world, becomes controlled by Sarlak, then our real world will become more evil. You won't notice a difference at first, but after a while, you will see that people are meaner, and no one will care about what's really important."

"Wow," Haley said.

"Yeah, wow," Uncle Johnny replied. "This is serious stuff. You need to stick together and use your strengths to fight off the Gorgons. Then we have to find a way to convince Lord D'Raygon that he is wrong, that he is being controlled. None of this will be easy."

"We're ready," Haley said.

"And Haley will lead us," Braden added. Everyone else nodded in agreement.

"Sure?" Uncle Johnny asked.

Haley looked at her brother and cousins. "Yes. Let's get rid of these smelly Gorgons."

Uncle Johnny chuckled. "It's only their breath that stinks."

Chapter Five

All the kids were ready to get out of that cramped basement. They had been down there for way too long and they really wanted to get some fresh air, at least. They packed all of the food and drinks into the backpack, and even found a pouch where they could put Uncle Johnny while they walked. Haley put the backpack on.

They walked to the top of the steps and stopped, knowing that they wouldn't be able to get past.

"Okay, once I clear that security gate, there is no turning back. We'll have to deal with whatever is out there and most likely, things are going to happen pretty quickly. Any questions?"

Jack raised his hand.

"You're not in school," Haley said.

"What Jack?" Uncle Johnny asked.

"You never told us something."

"What?"

"Why us?"

"Yeah," Braden added, "why were we picked to do this?"

"Because it runs in your family, that's why."

"What do you mean?"

"I'm not allowed to tell you too much about that yet, but all I can say is that you guys are not the first ones in your family to get signed up for this."

"You mean like our parents?" Jillian asked. "Why didn't they tell us anything?"

"I can't say who. I'm sorry. All I can say is that I am your uncle and I am one of them. Other than that, I have to keep it a secret, for now. Later, I will tell you whatever you want to know, okay?"

Everyone nodded.

"Anything else?"

"Is it going to be dangerous?" Haley asked.

"Probably. But if we stick together, we'll be okay. All we have to do is turn back this first wave of Gorgons and hopefully find a way to convince the Lord that he is being tricked. He's very angry right now. We have to at least fight off this first wave. That's what's most important."

"How are we going to do that?" Jillian asked.

"I'm not sure. You guys will have to think of something. Now, remember, trust each other, listen to me, and don't get scared. We will be fine. Let's go."

The ground rumbled a little bit and a bright light flashed at everyone's eyes quickly. To Jillian, the light was so bright it almost hurt, but it was too quick to really feel anything. It was like when her brother shined a flashlight in her eyes.

"Alright, we are ready to go outside," Uncle Johnny said. "Be ready. Things are a little different around here, so it won't look the same as it normally does. Don't worry about it, though."

Everyone walked into the hallway. Things seemed normal enough there. The black and white tile was on the floor, the staircase going up into the living room was still brown, and the cage for the dogs, Wyatt and Doc, was where it always was, against the wall to their left.

The front door was ahead of them, as was the window to the left. It was the kind of window that you really couldn't see out of because it had a design in it that made things seem blurry. All Jack could tell was that it was light outside. He couldn't remember if it was that way before they fell asleep.

Haley went toward the door. Everyone held their breath, even though they didn't know why. They had no idea what would be beyond that door. They were both excited and a little nervous. After all, none of them had been through something like this before.

Haley opened the door and again there was another bright light, this one coming from the sun. Everyone had to adjust their eyes after coming from the darker basement. Haley then opened the screen door, which made the same squeaky noise it always did, and stepped out onto the porch.

Once everyone got onto the porch, the door to the house closed by itself. This shocked everyone and Jillian let out a small scream.

"It's no big deal," Uncle Johnny said, "I should have told you about that."

"About what?" Braden asked.

"Well, you'll see. Let's just step off the porch first."

Haley stepped off the porch first, and she noticed something she hadn't before. The front of the house was not the same. As a matter of fact, it wasn't the front of the house at all. It was a huge open field of grass, with one tree all the way out in the distance.

"Um, Uncle Johnny?" she whispered behind her.

"Yes?"

"Where are we?"

"Wait for everyone else. I haven't shown that to them yet."

"Shown them?"

"It was sort of an illusion, a magic trick. I didn't want to frighten them, but I figured you could deal with it."

Haley wasn't so sure she could deal with it, but she said, "Okay."

Everyone else stepped off the porch and gathered around where Haley was standing. She paid attention and noticed that it looked like they were following the path of the walkway up to the house, which curved to her left. They must have really been seeing that. To her, there was nothing but open fields. Even the house was gone. She started to feel a little scared but fought it. She was the oldest, after all.

"Okay guys. Now is the time for the shocker. I want everyone to turn around and look at the house."

They all turned around, and by the time they were facing the house, it was gone. It just vanished, like it was never there.

"Wow," Jillian said.

"What happened?" Jack asked.

"We were never really in that house. It was just an illusion we created to make you feel comfortable. Remember, I said this place is like Earth but it is also not. This is a different place, and what we have to do is somewhere else."

"That's kind of cool," Braden said.

"Yeah, but that also means we can't go back to the house, right?" Jack asked.

"Pretty much," Uncle Johnny answered.

"But I could think of the house and make it appear, can't I?" Jillian asked.

"Not really. I don't think you've gotten that good yet."

"I could try," Jillian insisted. She wanted to think about it and make it appear right then. She wasn't sure if Uncle Johnny would be happy about that.

"But there's no need to waste your time on that. The Gorgons need to be dealt with, and Lord D'Raygon too. Let's work on them first, then we'll see what sort of neat tricks you can pull, okay?"

"Okay."

Braden looked at the open fields and wondered where they were. They could be anywhere, like another state, or even another country. He liked geography so he really wanted to know exactly where they were but he knew better than to ask that question. Instead, he pretended they were in Ireland, because he had seen pictures of Ireland where there were a lot of grassy open fields.

"Now, I need to transport us to our destination. It's gonna feel kinda funny and you might get dizzy but try not to let it bother you. The Gorgons will be close and you'll need to be ready."

"Okay," Haley and the rest of the kids said. Haley couldn't wait to get started. She wanted to use her power.

Jack couldn't wait either. He was the only one who didn't get a chance to really test out his power. He wanted to see how fast he could run. He held Gabby, careful not to look into her eyes. He didn't want to have to do something else for her again.

Chapter Six

Jillian knew Uncle Johnny said she might get dizzy, but this was more than that. First it looked like they were getting closer to the sky, like they were racing toward it. Then, the bottom dropped out and she felt like she was falling, fast. The only thing that stopped her from believing that was she didn't feel her hair moving or wind rushing at her face. They *felt* like they were moving really fast, but they weren't. Something else was going on, but Jillian couldn't figure out what it was.

She saw things flashing in front of her and she wanted to close her eyes but she was afraid she'd get even dizzier, maybe even sick. She certainly didn't want that. She just wanted it to end soon.

Like Uncle Johnny had heard what she was thinking, everything slowed down, to the point where she could see buildings and streets they were headed toward, and then it all stopped, finally.

"We're here," Uncle Johnny said.

"About time," Haley said. Jillian felt better knowing she wasn't the only one who felt that way.

"Yeah, I was about to throw up," Braden said.

"Me too," added Jack.

Jillian decided not to say anything.

"Okay, you see those buildings over there? The Gorgons are most likely right behind them. We have to plan something, but it will be tough to know exactly what they will do when they see us. If possible, we don't want to be attacked. I don't know if that is possible, though," Uncle Johnny said.

"Why don't we just blast 'em?" Jack asked, "You know, use our powers and wipe them out?"

"We could try, but right now we don't know how many of them there are. Plus, sometimes it is better to avoid a fight. If we could get to Lord D'Raygon and make him see things the right way, he could call his fighters off and end this all right away."

"Where is he?" Jillian asked.

"We don't know. I was able to locate the Gorgons but not him. We're going to have to keep a lookout."

"What does he look like?" Haley asked. Braden was going to ask the exact same question.

"No one knows for sure. He looks different than a regular Gorgon, because although his father was a Gorgon, his mother was not. Some say she was the most beautiful woman in the galaxy, maybe the universe. But no one knows what D'Raygon really looks like. He might look different since Sarlak has turned him evil." Jillian tried to picture what the son of a monster and a beautiful woman would look like but she couldn't really do it.

"He's evil now?" Braden asked.

"I wouldn't say evil just yet, but he's headed there."

"I thought you said the Gorgons were ugly," Haley said.

"Well, I guess that depends on how you look at it."

"That means they are ugly," Haley said.

"Maybe."

"So, how come we don't know what he looks like?" Jack asked.

"His birth was hidden at first because he wasn't a true Gorgon, and then Sarlak took over…wait."

"What's the matter?" Braden asked.

"Oh, no. Uh, something's going on here."

"Is something wrong? Are the Gorgons coming now?" Haley asked.

"No, not that. I feel something warm. Something warm and wet. Say, what did you tell me this doll can do?" Uncle Johnny asked. His voice was high-pitched, like he was really bothered by something.

"Um, a few things," Haley said, before anyone else could say something.

"Well, I think this doll has a leak, because I feel wet right now. Really wet. I also feel like I am going to—"

With that Uncle Johnny burst into tears again. He was crying loud too, and Jillian took him from the backpack.

"It's okay Uncle Johnny. You're in Baby-Wets- A Lot'. She can cry and she goes wee-wee. That's why I said you needed the diaper."

"I am a crying, wee-wee baby?" Uncle Johnny asked through tears. "Those are the special things I can do?"

The kids could barely understand what he was saying because he was crying so hard.

"It's not that bad," Haley said. "At least you won't scare the Gorgons away."

Jack and Braden laughed. Haley hadn't meant for her comment to be funny, but she realized it was, and she laughed a little too. Uncle Johnny didn't find it funny at all.

"Now you guys are laughing at me too. I am just a useless baby," he said, crying even harder.

"Baby-Wets-A-Lot only does this for a little while and then it stops. It won't be too bad," Jillian said, "and the diaper will keep you dry."

That didn't stop Uncle Johnny's crying. As a matter of fact, it made it worse. He seemed uncontrollable. Haley knew she had to do something.

"Uncle Johnny, you need to calm down. We need you. We don't know what to to!" she said.

"I-I-I'm trying," Uncle Johnny said, through tears. "It's not me, it's the doll. I am doing my best to control it."

"Try harder," Jack said.

"Do you know how hard this is?" Uncle Johnny said, crying harder again. "I'm stuck in this doll and I am going wee-wee in a diaper."

Braden and Jack started laughing. Haley gave them a look that told them to stop. She glared her eyes at them and frowned. They stopped.

"Now, Uncle Johnny, we need to know what to do. Are you okay?"

He made a sniffling sound. "I think so. I don't know what came over me. It must be the doll. Every time I get excited I feel like crying. I am sorry guys. I will try to not let that happen."

"It's okay, Uncle Johnny, it happens to me sometimes," Jillian said.

"Okay. The Gorgons are behind those two buildings over there."

The kids looked and saw two identical buildings. They weren't that tall, and they were made of red brick. They didn't seem much different than the ones they saw in the real world.

"What do they look like?" Jack asked.

"Like I said, they are seven feet tall, and pretty wide too. They look more like animals than people, but they can talk. They are hairy. I guess you could say they look like really big cavemen," Uncle Johnny said.

"Cavemen?" Jillian said.

"Yeah, those hairy guys you see in museums," Braden said.

"I think they are on TV commercials too," Haley said.

"Oh, I think I know what you are talking about now," Jillian said.

Then music started to play. It wasn't scary music at all, more like bells. Haley thought she recognized the sound, as did Jillian. Jack and Braden, however, knew exactly what it was.

"Ice cream!" they both said out loud and instantly they ran toward a white truck that had just appeared in the distance, not far away from the buildings Uncle Johnny had been talking about.

"Braden, Jack, stop!" Uncle Johnny yelled, but it was too late, they were too far away to hear him.

"What are they doing?" Haley asked.

"They are running right into trouble. Jillian?"

"Yes, Uncle Johnny?"

"In the mood for ice cream, are we?"

"Yes, but I didn't mean to make that truck appear. It just popped into my head."

"Any time you think of something you want, and tell yourself you really want it, it's going to appear."

"I'm sorry," Jillian said.

"It's okay. Now you know."

"What's the big deal about them going and getting ice cream from that truck?" Haley asked. She could go for some ice cream too. It was hot.

"There's no ice cream on that truck. It's full of Gorgons. They can sense when you use your abilities, especially with the help of Sarlak. It's a trap, and Braden and Jack are running right into it."

"We have to do something," Jillian said, "or it's all my fault."

"Yes, but what? What can we do Uncle Johnny?"

"Well, that's where my help kinda runs dry. I can't tell you what to do, it's part of the test, you could say."

"Well, that's a big help," Jillian said. Then she remembered Uncle Johnny's crying. She didn't want to go through that again. "But it's not your fault, it's the fault of whoever made the rules."

Haley tried to think. She looked at Braden and Jack and realized they were almost halfway to the truck already. Jack obviously wasn't running as fast as he could because Braden was keeping up with him. She had to do something fast, though.

"We can't ask for help, but can we ask about our powers?" she asked.

"All you want."

"Well, I can leap, but Jillian can't. Can I make her leap with me if I hold her hand?"

"Good question, and yes, you can. You just have to keep her in your mind. It should be pretty easy."

"Okay, so we'll leap over to them and stop them from getting to that truck."

"Sounds like a good idea to me," Jillian said. She had an idea too. She had to be careful; she had already made a mistake with the ice cream truck and she didn't want to make a mistake again.

Haley grabbed a hold of Gabby and Jillian had the backpack with Uncle Johnny in it. They held hands and were about to start running.

"I have an idea. Just start running. You'll see it when it comes."

"Okay," Haley said and they took off. They were running pretty fast, but they could see that Braden and Jack were getting really close to that truck in the distance. Jillian didn't know what a Gorgon was or what one looked like but she had a feeling she didn't want to know and she certainly didn't want her brother or cousin being attacked by one.

She closed her eyes and thought hard. In the distance, a large trampoline appeared, just like the one in Haley and Jack's backyard. It was about 20 feet away.

"Great idea," Haley said. "I'll bounce us off of that and we should get there twice as fast."

Haley did just that. She took a small leap, making sure to remember she had a hold of Jillian's hand, and bounced them off the trampoline.

They soared high in the air, higher than any of them had ever soared before. Jillian could feel it in her stomach. It reminded her of being on a Ferris wheel, or a roller coaster. Gabby just giggled. It seemed she liked being high up in the air.

Haley was pretty sure she had timed the jump correctly. It should land them right in between the truck and the boys. Hopefully, once they landed, she could talk some sense into them.

Chapter Seven

Jillian figured this was what it must feel like to fly. They had bounced off the trampoline and soared through the air. She could feel the wind rush against her face as they got closer and closer to where the boys were running. She didn't understand why they ran off like that and she felt kind of guilty about it. She wanted to tell herself it wasn't her fault but that was hard to do.

Haley focused on the ground, which was coming at them pretty fast. She hoped she could land them safely. After all, Jillian and Gabby were her responsibility. She didn't want to make a mistake and get someone hurt.

Haley braced herself for the landing and yelled out for Jillian to do the same. The ground was dusty, kind of like the dirt on a baseball field, and soft. They landed, and didn't fall. Haley figured she was lucky. So did Jillian. Gabby just kept laughing.

Braden and Jack were only ten feet away when they landed and Uncle Johnny screamed out, "Stop!" It was so loud the sound rang in Haley's ears. But it worked. The boys stopped.

"We just wanted some ice cream," Braden said.

"There's no ice cream in there, just Gorgons," Uncle Johnny answered.

"What?" Jack asked.

"It's a trap, that's all it is. They want you to go there so they can attack you. It's called divide and conquer. Instead of fighting a whole group, they fight you in smaller numbers so they can win."

"That's not very fair," Braden said.

"Nothing is going to be fair here," Uncle Johnny said, "and it would be good if you remembered to stick with the group. Running off like that was wrong. The both of you."

"I'm sorry," Jack and Braden said at the same time. To Haley, it seemed like they really meant it. She'd seen Jack lie about being sorry before.

"Sorry doesn't cut it this time, guys," Uncle Johnny said. No one had ever heard him so angry before. "You put everyone at risk for something you wanted. That's not right and it won't be tolerated any more, understand?"

"Yes," the boys answered.

"Are you sure?"

"We're sure."

"Then make sure it doesn't happen again. This is a very serious situation and we need you to get this job done and get it done right."

"Okay," everyone answered.

Uncle Johnny explained that the Gorgon stronghold was just beyond the two buildings. He also told Jillian to wish away the ice cream truck. When she did, it disappeared, along with the Gorgons inside of it.

The kids needed to come up with a plan, something to defeat the Gorgons and save everyone. It seemed like a big task, maybe too big for a group of kids, Haley thought.

Braden didn't doubt. He knew there had to be a way they could beat these guys and he put his mind to work at figuring out the solution. Jack did the same, trying to pretend this was a video game. He was good at those. If he treated this like a game, maybe he could make everything work out.

No one saw it coming. No one expected it. The Gorgons must have sensed that the kids were busy thinking and not paying attention because they launched a sneak attack. Uncle Johnny never even got a chance to shout out a warning, things happened so fast.

The Gorgons didn't just have size on their side, they had weapons. One of their weapons was a cannon that shot out blasts of air. Maybe that doesn't sound so dangerous, but the Gorgons had found a way to harness the power of forced air so well they could knock down huge buildings with it.

They had fired the cannon at the kids. Thankfully, it wasn't on the highest setting. Still, it was enough to knock the breath out of all of them and send them flying in the air as if there was a big explosion.

Haley landed on her stomach, totally surprised by the attack. She didn't know what hit her and the rest of them, but she knew she was hurt and took a while to get up. The first thing she did was look for Gabby. Gabby had landed on her back and seemed to be fine. She was laughing again, though Haley had no idea how she could be.

What scared her was she couldn't see anyone else.

Jack landed on his side, and his arm hurt. He also didn't know what hit him. His neck also hurt. It felt like he was thrown a hundred feet, maybe more.

He got up slowly, dusted himself off and looked for everyone else. All he saw was a big cloud of dust. No one was around. He felt that feeling in his stomach he got when he was scared or nervous. He tried to control it, but it took over.

Before it got too bad, he heard a voice. It sounded like a boy, but it wasn't a voice he had ever heard before.

"Everything's okay," the boy said, "you just got the wind knocked out of you."

"Who are you?" Jack asked.

"Now's not the time for that." The boy's voice was forceful, like an adult's. "You need to act quickly. They will strike again otherwise."

"Where's Uncle Johnny?"

"Don't worry about him now. Your sister and cousins are to your left. Braden is only ten or so feet in front of you. Run to him, and then get to your sister. You guys have to make a move. Everything will be fine if you do."

"Okay," Jack said, not really sure if everything really was okay.

"Do it now, and don't tell anyone you spoke to me," the boy said. He didn't yell, and he didn't sound mean, but he sure sounded like he meant business, so Jack did what he said.

Braden didn't know where he was. A minute ago, they were running toward the ice cream truck, then all of a sudden, he was on his back looking up at the sky through a large cloud of dust. He tried to breathe but his lungs hurt when he did. This wasn't good at all.

Like Jack, he started to get scared but he tried to control it. His mother always told him he could fight his fear if he wanted to; he just needed to want to.

It wasn't so easy this time.

Before he really got scared, he saw someone come toward him. He realized it was Jack and he got himself to his feet. No need for anyone to see him lying down like that.

Jack didn't even stop running before he said, "We gotta move."

"Where to?" Braden asked. He would have preferred to wait a bit to catch his breath.

"They're gonna strike again, real soon. We have to get to Haley and Jillian and Gabby,"

"Where are they?"

Jack pointed in the direction the boy told him.

"How do you know?" Braden asked.

Jack remembered a line the boy said and it seemed like the right time to use it. "Now's not the time," he said, copying the forceful tone the boy had used with him.

"Huh?"

"Just follow me," Jack said. "And trust me. I haven't done you wrong yet."

Braden was a little confused, but Jack seemed to know what he was talking about and considering everything else that was going on, that was fine by him. If something went wrong, at least it would be someone else's fault.

Jack and Braden ran as fast as they could. Without running at top speed, to Jack it seemed to take forever to get to them. Braden tried not to doubt Jack. Jack had been right, he hadn't done him wrong yet.

About halfway there, Braden yelled out, "Stop!"

"We can't stop now, we have to—" Jack cut off his words when he saw what was in Braden's hand; the head of Baby-Wets-A-Lot.

"Oh, no," Jack said.

"You got that right. Without Uncle Johnny, what are we going to do?"

"You are going to get to your sister," the boy said to Jack, "and you are going to do it fast."

"Did you hear that?" Jack asked.

"What?"

"Nothing. Come on, let's go. We'll talk to Haley and see what we have to do."

They started running again, both of them knowing they were in trouble without the help of Uncle Johnny.

Chapter Eight

"What are we going to do?" Haley asked when she saw Jack holding the doll's head. "Uncle Johnny was supposed to be the one to help us, now he is gone."

No one said anything at first. Instead, they all tried to fight back the fear they felt. It was bad enough that they were supposed to fight the Gorgons, creatures they never even heard of before, but to have to do it without their guide? That was near impossible.

"Maybe this is part of the test," Braden said.

"What test?" Jillian asked.

"The test Uncle Johnny kept talking about. Maybe this is part of it. Maybe we are supposed to see if we can work together without him."

"He's right," Jack said, "this part of the test is to probably see what we do when things look bad. And this looks pretty bad."

"You have a point. So, what do we do now?" Haley asked.

Braden and Jack didn't have a quick answer to that. In the distance, they heard a rumbling sound, coming from behind the buildings. It almost sounded like the buildings were going to come crashing down it was so loud.

"I think they are getting ready," Jillian said.

Jack remembered what the boy had said to him. "We don't have much time. We have to do something, and do it fast," he said.

Everyone nodded. Haley wondered what they were going to do. Then, it came to her. "We have to find a way to work together. That's what this test is all about. We have to combine our powers and win this battle."

"How?" Braden asked.

After thinking for a moment, it seemed so obvious to Haley. "You and Jillian are brother and sister, and so are me and Jack. We should try and combine our powers that way first. It makes the most sense to me."

Considering no one else had a better idea, there were no arguments. Jillian had a question, though. "What about Gabby?"

"I think she'll use her power when the time comes for that," Braden said. That , too, made sense to everyone. It must have made sense to Gabby as well because she giggled.

"Like Jack said, we don't have time. So Haley, you and Jack should leap and run over to those buildings and see what we are up against. Then Jillian and I will come up with a way to combine our powers and launch an attack on the Gorgons. What do you say?"

Jack shrugged his shoulders. "Why not? You okay with that?" he asked Haley.

"Like you said, why not?"

Jack and Haley took off, Jack kicking up dust and dirt behind him and Haley leaping into the air like a superhero. That left Braden, Jillian, and Gabby alone. For a moment, Braden started to rethink how good his plan was.

If you've never seen a Gorgon up close, and not many people have, it surely isn't a pleasant sight. Gorgons are tall, and hairy. On top of that, they have no visible lips, so their teeth are always showing. Those teeth are big and pointy, too. They are almost as funny looking as they are scary, but it certainly isn't recommended to let them know that.

Haley noticed this when she landed on the top of the building on the right. The Gorgons couldn't see her but she could see them. She saw three groups of six of them. All of them were holding clubs, and one group controlled the big air gun they had used earlier. The gun was big, with a long silver barrel. It reminded Haley of something she saw in history class, a cannon like the ones used in the Civil War, only this one was bigger.

Jack saw the Gorgons too, and he nearly froze when he did. From the ground, they were huge. Each of them wore what looked like space suits made out of animal skins. The clubs they carried were almost as big as Jack himself and he decided right then he didn't want to be hit by one of them.

Jack looked up and saw Haley on the roof. She motioned to him that they should go back and he had no problem with that plan. He raced back, trying to beat his sister to safety.

Braden saw his cousins approaching and he couldn't wait for them to get to him. He and Jillian had come up with a plan. It might not have been perfect, but he figured it was the best they could do under the circumstances.

After he told them the plan, Haley said, "That just might work. But what are Jack and I going to do?"

"While we launch the attack, you take Gabby and start thinking of how to get Jack's other powers to come out," Braden said.

"Other powers?" Jack asked.

"I know what he is talking about. The anger and fear powers Uncle Johnny said we have to be careful with."

"Now might be a time when we are supposed to use them."

"But I don't know what mine is," Jack said.

"That's what we'll figure out." Haley turned to Braden. "You guys get into position. I'll take Jack and Gabby to the roof of the building on the right. I saw the perfect safe place there. I'll let you know when we figure out Jack's other powers."

"Okay. It's time to move," Braden said. "Do you remember the stuff you are supposed to make appear, Jillian?"

"I think so. Galaxy Slime?"

"Galaxy Gemstone Slime, the stuff I yelled at you for opening last Christmas."

"Oh, that slime. I remember that. It had sparkles in it."

"That's the stuff," Braden said.

"Okay guys, we all know what to do," Haley said. "Good luck."

"Good luck," everyone replied, and they went their separate ways, hoping that what Uncle Johnny had told and taught them was enough.

Without saying it, each one worried about Uncle Johnny, wondering where he might be at what was the most dangerous time of their lives.

Chapter Nine

My other powers, Jack thought, what are they? It seemed like everyone else had theirs figured out and he was holding them up. He needed to think, to concentrate. It was like in school, the teacher would talk and Jack would try to concentrate. There was always something else on his mind.

He decided right then he would stop it.

Haley took his hand and he held onto Gabby as hard as he could with the other. All of this just didn't seem real, all this stuff about powers and Gorgons and saving the world. Maybe it was just a dream and only he was experiencing it.

"You ready?" Haley asked.

"I guess so."

Haley chuckled. "I guess none of us really are. Here we go."

Haley and Jack started running, Jack making sure not to run too fast. The dust kicked up around them. Jack heard a rumbling from somewhere behind the buildings. The Gorgons were readying their next attack. He had to find his other powers before it was too late.

Haley bent down while running and yelled "Hold on!"

With that she leaped, taking Jack and Gabby with her. They were almost flying through the air. Jack couldn't believe it.

Ahead of them, the building on the right approached, and fast. Jack was a little scared, but he trusted his sister. He really had no choice. Uncle Johnny had told them it was what they needed to do.

They landed with a thud, and Jack felt just a little pain in his ankles but that was it. Haley had landed them right next to a huge metal box that Jack recognized as an air conditioner; his father had told him what they were not so long before.

Thinking about his father, and then his mother, made Jack a little scared. Where were they? Did they know what was happening? Would they be okay? He didn't know the answers and thought maybe he didn't want to.

The fear he felt made his face feel cold. He'd felt something like that before when he was scared. He told himself to control his fear.

"No," the boy's voice told him. "You need to give into your fear." The voice was more forceful than before.

"But Uncle Johnny said not to, he said it was dangerous."

"Not all rules are true all the time. Sometimes you have to bend them, or break them, to get done what you need to."

"Who are you?" Jack asked.

"Not now. Now, you just have to trust me. Did I help you before?"

"Yes," Jack answered.

"This one will be harder. But you have to trust. Do you?"

"I don't know."

"There is no time for I don't know," the boy said, this time sounding like he was losing his patience. "You have to trust me. All of your lives depend on it. Your sister's life depends on it."

"Okay," Jack said. He didn't want to be responsible for anyone else getting hurt. He'd do what the boy told him. After all, he was right the first time,

"Okay, what I am about to tell you do to might seem crazy…"

The Gorgons were coming. They had arranged themselves in battle formation and were prepared to make their move. They didn't have powers like the Dream Fighters so they needed to use their physical strength instead, and they had plenty of that. They were known around the galaxy for their strength.

The first part of the Dream Fighters' plan had worked, the Gorgons did not know Haley and Jack and Gabby had moved to the top of the building. The Gorgons would make their attack where Braden and Jillian stood, seemingly unarmed and weak.

"They're coming," Jillian said.

"I don't see them."

"I can feel them. They are ready to go," Jillian insisted.

Braden thought maybe Jillian was making it up but after what they all had gone through, he was willing to give her the benefit of the doubt. Maybe she could feel them. Anything seemed possible.

"You know what to do?"

"I think so."

"Don't think. Be sure."

Jillian did not want to let her brother down. "Okay."

"Let's do this. Whenever you are ready."

Jillian closed her eyes and thought back to that Christmas. Sure, Braden yelled at her a lot, like most big brothers do, but she was pretty sure she remembered the toy he was talking about. She concentrated like Uncle Johnny taught her and made something appear.

In front of Braden appeared a container of Galaxy Slime. "Okay, you're close. You brought it to me in the box. I need it out of the box so I can put it all together in one big ball."

Normally, Braden might have lost his patience with Jillian but this time he didn't, he actually said it nice. That inspired Jillian. Maybe she could make up for bringing the ice cream truck.

"How about this?" she said, closing her eyes and picturing a big blob of the galaxy slime.

A huge blob appeared in front of Braden. It was over ten feet wide and almost the exact size he was thinking of using.

"Great job," he said, and then he pointed his hands toward the blob and raised it in the air. Uncle Johnny had told him that the size of what he could move with his mind didn't matter. He believed him and the ball stayed in front of him, suspended.

"Wow," Jillian said, "We did it."

"Not so fast. We have to make sure part two works."

Braden built up as much energy in his mind as he could. He could feel the heat in his fingertips.

"Hey, Gorgons, eat this!" he said and he launched the huge blob of Galaxy Slime toward the spot where Haley and Jack said the Gorgons were hiding.

The blob flew through the air, flattening a little bit from the speed, but holding together. Braden had worried it might fall apart.

The blob was moving fast, maybe 50 miles an hour, and it raced toward the Gorgon hideout. It seemed to be right on course, but it smashed into the left building, splattering all over the place.

"Darn," Braden said.

"That's a bad word," Jillian said.

"No it's not. "

"Well, it's not a good word."

"Okay, maybe it isn't. I'm just mad because I forgot to calculate the wind. I know better than that. Can you do it again?"

"Of course," Jillian said, as if it were nothing. "But we better move quick. They know where that came from."

"Go."

Another big ball of Galaxy slime appeared, this one even bigger than the last. Braden lifted it and launched it even faster at his target, this time aiming higher and more to the right so it would drop right on the Gorgons.

He nailed it. The blob landed right in the middle of the Gorgon army, covering half of them in the sticky goo. It didn't hurt them but it would slow them down.

"You hit them," Jillian said, I can see it in my mind."

"Great. Let's keep doing it. We'll hold them back until someone comes up with a way to stop them."

Chapter Ten

Haley had finally calmed Gabby down, who didn't want to sit still at all. She kept trying to get up and a few times she said "Leave." Haley didn't want to stay there either but she knew it was the safest place for them to be.

"Building go boom," Gabby said.

"Boom?"

Gabby nodded. "Leave."

"No Gabby, we can't leave. Not until Braden finishes and Jack finds his power. Then we can leave."

Gabby didn't seem happy with that answer but Haley knew they had no choice. She wished this was all over already. Sure it was great to have powers, but with Uncle Johnny gone, this really wasn't fun anymore.

"I am not gone," Uncle Johnny said. Haley looked around for the doll but it was nowhere to be found.

"Where are you?"

"I can't explain that. I can talk to you through your mind. You don't have to speak, just think, and I will hear you."

"What happened?"

"The destruction of the doll forced me away. It doesn't matter; it's better this way anyway."

"Okay," Haley said. "What should we do now?"

"Keep doing what you are doing. Trust each other and work together. You're doing fine."

"Are you sure? I feel like we don't know what to do next."

Uncle Johnny laughed. "No one really does. We just try to prepare ourselves and hope we make the right decisions when the time comes. That's really it."

"Gabby said this building is going to go boom," Haley said.

"Maybe you should listen to her. But first you need to help Jack find his power."

Haley turned around and looked at Jack.

Jack walked toward the edge of the building and looked down. It looked like he shook his head a few times. Then, out of nowhere, he jumped...

"Feel it, feel the fear run through you from your head to your toes," the boy told Jack. "We are all given fear to help protect us. It helps us run faster and make quick decisions when we need to."

"I'm scared," Jack said.

"Good. Feel it."

Jack felt his face get colder and colder. He thought it was just the wind blowing against it. This was a little different though. He felt like he dunked his head in ice cold water.

The ground rushed toward him, and he saw a huge multi-colored blob rush underneath him and crash into a large group of Gorgons, splattering them with goo.

Jack was going to land right amongst them if he didn't stop or someone didn't save him. He didn't know why he listened to the boy. It looked like he had made a huge mistake and he got more scared, making his face even colder. It felt like when he stayed out too long in the winter snow. It was so cold it hurt.

Haley saw Jack jump off the building and panicked. Uncle Johnny was saying something in her head but she didn't listen. Instead, she grabbed Gabby and in what looked like a streak of light, she bolted toward the edge of the building and sailed off, like a bird.

She raced toward her brother, who was falling fast. He was more than halfway to the ground and the Gorgons.

Haley didn't know what they would do if they had to fight the Gorgons head on. They would lose.

She told herself that wasn't going to happen.

With a mixture of confidence and good old fear, Haley streaked through the air toward Jack. She grabbed him with her left arm and held him tight.

Before Haley got to him, Jack felt a surge of coldness run through his whole body.

"Good, you've got it. Now, let it go."

"What do you mean?"

"You're going to crash, Jack. It's going to hurt worse than anything you've ever felt before. You're going to let everyone down."

"No!" Jack yelled, feeling anger replace some of the fear.

Then, he felt an arm around him. He turned to look at the Gorgons, who saw him coming and were getting ready. Most of them were covered with slime and looked ridiculous.

Two blue bolts shot out of Jack's eyes and went directly toward the Gorgons and another Galaxy Slime ball heading toward them. The bolts froze everything in their path. The Gorgons that got caught in the bolt's range stopped in their tracks, and were then knocked over by the frozen Galaxy Slime ball Braden had launched at them. The Gorgons were cut in half by the attack and retreated about a hundred feet behind them. Jack's face felt normal again.

Haley landed softly, with Gabby and Jack in her arms. This leap wasn't really a leap, it was more like flying. She didn't know where it came from or whether or not she could do it again. She hoped she didn't have to.

"Good job," the boy said to Jack.

"What were you thinking?" Haley asked.

"It was the only way I could get my fear power to come out."

"You almost hurt yourself bad."

"It was a risk I had to take," Jack said, repeating what the boy had told him.

"Haley and Jack are in trouble," Jillian said. "So is Gabby."

"What do you mean," Braden asked.

"I can *feel* it. Something's gonna happen. The Gorgons are coming for them."

Though he couldn't feel it exactly the way his sister could, Braden did feel that something bad was going to happen. In the distance, he could see the three of them. They were right between the two buildings. He wanted to call out to them to get them to escape but he knew they couldn't hear.

"You have to go to them," Uncle Johnny said in Braden's head. "It's going to be up to you this time. Otherwise, they'll be trapped."

"Uncle Johnny, you're back!"

"Not exactly. But I can see what is going on and I can talk to you, at least for now."

"What should I do?" Braden asked.

"Who are you talking to?" Jillian asked.

"Uncle Johnny, shh."

"Uncle Johnny? He's back?"

"He's in my head," Braden said.

"And yours too, Jillian." Uncle Johnny was now talking to both of them. "You can't bring your cousins over here. You have to fight the Gorgons over there."

"But how?" Braden asked.

"That's up to you. I can't help there. Just find a way to combine your powers and defeat the Gorgons here once and for all."

"They are *not* ready," a voice said, the same boy's voice Jack had heard before.

"We will never know," Uncle Johnny said, "and now is not the time to argue about it."

"You can't send them in there unprepared."

"I prepared them the best I could."

"Did you? I had to help Jack find his other power, and Jillian doesn't know hers yet."

"Who are you?" Jillian asked.

"Not the time for that. Jillian," the boy said. "But I promise to properly introduce myself when the time comes."

"They have to make a move now. Braden, it's up to you. Haley and Jack and Gabby are about to get ambushed. You can't let that happen."

Braden thought for a minute. "Maybe I do have to let it happen."

"What do you mean?"

"You'll see."

"They are not ready," the boy said again.

"We'll just have to find out," Braden answered, "won't we."

Chapter Eleven

Braden discussed his plan with Jillian, telling her that she should wait where she was. Jillian resisted at first, but Braden told her that they needed someone to stay in a safe place where everyone could meet after Braden acted out his plan.

After he was done explaining, Braden ran toward where Haley and Jack were, hoping he could get there in time.

"You'll make it, the Gorgons haven't started moving," Jillian said in his head.

"How are you doing that?"

"I don't know. I just thought it and you heard it. Pretty cool, huh?"

"Yeah, very. Alright, let's hope this works."

Jack was shocked by what he had done. He now knew why his face felt cold when he was afraid. It was crazy to jump off the building, but the boy must have known that Haley would save him.

And what about what Haley did? She actually flew, like a superhero. So many things were happening to them; so many different powers were being found. This was crazier than anything Jack had experienced before.

"What do we do now?" Haley asked.

"I don't know. I think we might have stopped them for a bit. But we have to do better than that."

"I know. But how?"

"Braden," Gabby said. "Braden coming."

"He is?" Jack asked.

Gabby nodded. "Building go boom."

"There she goes again with that," Haley said. "She said the same thing before and Uncle Johnny said she is probably right."

"When did you talk to Uncle Johnny and how?" Jack asked.

"Before you pulled your little birdie stunt off the building. He said he can still talk to us."

"Really? Uncle Johnny, can you hear me?"

There was no answer.

"Uncle Johnny?"

"I think he talks to us when he needs to. Maybe now he doesn't need to."

"That's not fair. I want to talk to him. I want him to tell us what to do," Jack said.

"He told me he can't help us that way. Maybe when Braden gets here we will figure it out."

Just then, Braden did show up. He was out of breath.

"I need one of your powers. This regular running just doesn't work," he said, panting.

"Maybe I can teach you," Jack said.

"It doesn't matter. Right now we have to worry about the Gorgons who are on their way over here."

"They are?"

"Yes."

"How do you know?" Jack asked.

"Think about it. Feel it."

Jack did. "I do feel it. I feel like when you say it, you're right. It's kind of weird."

"I feel it too," Haley said.

"Then you know we have to do something, and I have a plan."

"Where's Jillian?"

"Back where we were before. I figured one of us had to stay in a safe spot. Plus, we are going to need our powers and not hers right now."

"What do you have in mind?" Haley asked.

Braden told Haley and Jack his plan. It was absolutely dangerous and crazy, but they all figured it might just work.

"Do you guys think you can use those powers?"

"I have control of my running," Jack said.

"I think I can do the protective bubble again, especially if you are going to do what you are planning to do."

"All right. Now all we have to do is get those Gorgons to come over here. Jack, when I say so, you take Gabby and run right toward where Jillian is. Try to contact Uncle Johnny and find out if we can get out of here."

"Got it."

"And Haley, you put that protective bubble over us when Jack takes off. Got it?"

"I do."

"If we can do that, we should be able to pull this off."

Braden looked down and saw a large rock in front of him. He lifted the rock and launched it at where the Gorgons were. He did this several times and before they knew it, the ground starting shaking. About 20 Gorgons, way more than they figured they could fight head on, came toward them.

Braden's plan had better work, they all thought.

Chapter Twelve

Each one of them felt the fear inside them. The Gorgons were coming and they were huge. There was no way they could fight them, and in a way, Braden's plan seemed more dangerous than doing that. Neither option seemed to be the right one but it was all they had.

The massive Gorgons got closer. They were beasts, looking even bigger than they had before. Braden had never seen them up close and it shocked him as they approached. Even he was starting to doubt his plan. Right then, all of them wished they were back in the basement playing video games instead of fighting huge beasts.

When the Gorgons, who were rushing in a straight line at the kids, were within 50 feet, Braden said, "Okay, get ready. This won't work unless we wait until they are right on top of us, okay?"

"Got it," Jack and Haley both said, at the same time. They tried not to think about how dangerous this was and did their best to trust it would work.

The Gorgons were twenty feet away. The kids could feel the ground shaking below them. Dust flew in the air behind the wave of Gorgons. Jack felt his face get cold. No, he said to himself, now was not the time for his fear power. He squeezed Gabby tighter.

"Anger," the boy said. "You have to get angry."

"I know."

"Think of how these Gorgons want to hurt you and your sister and your cousins. Think of how unfair that is. You did nothing to them."

"I'm trying."

"Don't try. Do. There is no time for a mistake."

The Gorgons were now right on top of the kids, and raising their clubs high in the air as if they were going to smash the kids to pieces. Braden could smell them. He didn't smell the breath Uncle Johnny had mentioned. He just smelled the Gorgons themselves. It reminded him of when his dog came in from the rain.

Haley felt the fear rise up in her. She knew what needed to be done and was pretty sure she could do it. But would it be enough? Would the bubble that knocked Jack down back in the basement be able to protect them from what Braden was about to do?

Jack made sure he had a good grip on Gabby and looking at her, he got angry thinking the Gorgons would try to hurt a little girl. It worked.

They were right between the two buildings, and Braden raised both hands, pointing one at each of the buildings. He kept them there, concentrating like his uncle had taught him in the basement.

"Now!" he yelled.

Like a streak of lightning, Jack bolted away, toward where Jillian was, with Gabby under his arm.

Braden, in one smooth motion, brought his hands down, and the buildings started to fall toward them, like someone had blown them up. The noise was so loud. Haley couldn't even hear her thoughts.

Just before the Gorgons were able to bring their clubs down on them, the protective bubble appeared, and the clubs all bounced off.

The Gorgons weren't paying attention to the buildings behind them, and the bricks came down on them. Haley and Braden ducked down to the ground and heard the bricks bounce off the Gorgons and the protective bubble.

Jillian couldn't believe what she was seeing. A huge cloud of dust covered where Haley and Braden and the Gorgons had once stood. All of a sudden, she felt a fear she had never felt before. She wasn't sure why, but she punched the ground and it felt like the whole Earth shook. She had found her new power, strength, and she had a whole lot of it.

Jack arrived, holding Gabby under his arm.

"Boom," Gabby said.

"Yes, boom," Jack said, "you were right."

"Are they okay?" Jillian asked.

"I don't know. Braden told me to leave before he knocked the buildings down."

"Are you okay?" Jillian asked Braden in her head. He didn't answer. Jillian was afraid he and Haley had gotten hurt. "What do we do now?" she asked Jack.

"Braden said to try and contact Uncle Johnny."

"I've been trying, but he isn't answering."

"Yeah, I know. But we have to keep doing it."

Braden stood up. The protective bubble Haley created was gone, and there were bricks and rubble everywhere except for a small circle that surrounded Haley and him. Haley got up too. She looked very tired. Braden felt the same way, like knocking down those buildings took all his energy from him.

"You okay?" he asked Haley.

"Yeah, I am just weak."

"I think it worked."

They both looked around and saw no sign of the Gorgons. They must have been buried underneath the rubble. So, Braden's plan worked. Now they needed to find a way out.

"I think we should go find everyone."

"Braden, are you okay?" Jillian said.

"I'm fine," he answered in his mind.

"I think we should go too," Haley said.

"Good." Braden let Jillian know they were coming.

What none of them knew was that the Gorgons weren't nearly done.

Chapter Thirteen

Halfway through Haley's leap, she and Braden heard a huge engine sound, like an airplane. They looked behind them and saw three large aircraft, shaped like the flying dinosaurs Haley had seen in a museum. They didn't look exactly the same, these were made out of metal and had smoother shapes, but they were close. They were shiny silver and the sun reflected off them, almost blinding Haley and Braden.

One thing they knew for sure was that this spelled trouble. Fighting off Gorgons on the ground was one thing, but this was different. What were they going to do now?

Jack saw the ships first. Jillian had said something didn't feel right. The three ships were coming right at them. Jack tried to think of what they could do, but no ideas came right then. Maybe they should all run, he thought, but he didn't think he could run with Jillian and Gabby.

Before they had the chance to react, the Gorgons fired their cannon, sending a shock wave right at them. The wave blew Haley and Braden to the ground and scattered Jack, Jillian, and Gabby.

Not again, Jack thought. He got up, feeling aches all over his body. He looked around and saw Jillian about ten feet away from him. He didn't see Gabby anywhere.

. "Gorgon Warbirds," Uncle Johnny said so all of them could hear. "This is unexpected. You guys have to listen to me. Find each other."

"I'll try," Jack said.

"Get to Gabby first. She's not far from you, but the Gorgons are coming for her."

"I told you they weren't ready," the boy said.

"Not now," Uncle Johnny said. "Let's get them out of this."

Jack ran toward where Uncle Johnny told him Gabby was. Another blast hit the ground before him. This one was smaller and more concentrated, and it knocked him off his feet.

When he got up, he saw a Gorgon heading toward him. What he didn't know was that the Gorgon wasn't coming for him, he was going after Gabby.

Haley got up. Her head hurt. She didn't see anyone around her at first, but then saw Braden get up a few feet away. Not much further than that, she saw a Gorgon bend down and pick Gabby up.

"No!" she yelled, but that didn't stop anything. "Braden, they have Gabby."

"Oh, no. We have to do something."

When they went to move toward the Gorgon, another blast like the one fired at Jack exploded the ground in front of them. It wasn't so powerful, and it just knocked them down.

The Gorgon bent down and with his hairy hands picked Gabby up, who was sitting in the dirt after the first blast. The Gorgon's hand was about half the size of Gabby herself, and she tried to get away but couldn't.

The Gorgon took Gabby and started running away, toward where Braden had knocked the buildings down. Before he got halfway, he stopped. Then, he made a big mistake. He looked Gabby in the eyes.

"Aw, cute little girl," he said in a deep, scratchy voice.

Gabby locked on his eyes. "Go back," she said.

"Go back," the Gorgon said.

"Help Haley."

"Help Haley," the Gorgon repeated, and he started running toward where Haley and Braden were. Jack and Jillian were coming toward that spot as well.

Haley couldn't believe her eyes. Coming right at her was a huge Gorgon and a giggling Gabby. She then realized that Gabby must have used her power on the Gorgon and now he had to do whatever she wanted. She wasn't sure, but she figured this wasn't so safe.

"A Gorgon," Jack said.

"He's with Gabby," Haley said. "I think it's okay."

The Gorgon stopped and put Gabby down in front of Braden. "Help Haley," he said.

"Go back where you came from," Haley told the Gorgon but it didn't seem like he understood her.

"Help Haley," he said.

"Gabby, make him go back. You can't control him forever," Haley insisted. "And he is better off there than with us."

The Warbirds swooped down toward them and the Gorgon jumped in the air trying to hit one of them. They didn't fire, probably because they were confused at what was happened, but they circled, preparing for another strike.

"What are we going to do?"

"Go back," Gabby said to the Gorgon, and he listened, running toward where he came from.

"Maybe we can knock them out of the air with something," Braden said.

"Like what?" Jack asked,

"I really don't know. Uncle Johnny, can you help us here?"

There was no answer. Instead, the kids watched in fear as the Gorgon Warbirds approached. On each wing was a cannon, and the kids saw the cannons light up, as if they were going to fire something at them.

"Haley, can you make that bubble big enough to cover all of us?" Jack asked.

"I don't know. I don't think so. I barely got it big enough to cover me and Braden."

"I told you they weren't ready," the boy's voice said, this time for all of them to hear. "You didn't listen."

"They needed to be tested," Uncle Johnny answered, "and all of this wasn't my idea."

"Well, now we have to do something."

Underneath the Warbirds, a new group of Gorgons appeared and rushed toward the kids. There must have been twenty of them.

Without even thinking, Jack shot two bolts at them, but only one Gorgon was hit and he froze in place. The others didn't even react. They kept coming. It wouldn't be long before they reached the kids.

"Hang tight guys, I'm coming," they all heard Uncle Johnny say. None of them thought he would make it in time.

Then, out of nowhere, a boy appeared. They didn't really get a good look at him because he was moving so fast. It was more like a blur. He raced toward the group of Gorgons as if to try to stop them from getting to the kids.

In his right hand was what looked like a sword made of energy. He swung it so fast that all the kids could see were arcs of light. Gorgons were getting knocked in all directions, and the boy kept moving in such fast, fluid motions, no one could see his face.

Then, when most of the Gorgons on the ground were taken care of, he stopped. His back faced them. Haley could see that he was just a little taller than her, with blonde hair that came almost to his shoulders. He was wearing what looked like a black cloak.

He raised his left hand, and pointed it toward the Warbirds. Immediately, they stopped, staying still in the air. The Warbirds fired what looked like laser missiles at him but he countered by creating a huge bubble around him, just like what Haley could do. The lasers bounced off, not coming close to touching him.

Two Gorgons on the ground attacked and he quickly knocked them away with the sword. It happened so fast the kids almost missed it.

"Get them out of here already," the boy said in all of their heads.

With that, Uncle Johnny appeared behind the kids. He looked a little different than he did in real life. He seemed taller.

"Time to go guys," he said.

"Uncle Johnny!" all the kids screamed when they turned around.

"Let's get out of here. Everyone hold hands. Close your eyes."

They all listened. They felt themselves moving real fast. When they opened their eyes again, they were in a large room with what looked like computer monitors. They were standing in the back of room with Uncle Johnny.

"Where are we?" Jillian asked.

"The academy," Uncle Johnny answered.

"Academy?" Jack asked.

"Yes, this is where you guys will get your training."

"We left that boy all alone," Haley said.

"He can handle himself."

"Who was he?" Braden asked.

"I think it's best if he tells you that."

Uncle Johnny led them out of the room and into another one. This one looked like a lobby. There was a large statue of a man with a beard in the center of the room.

"What happened with the Gorgons? And Sarlak?" Jack asked.

"We fought off this attack. You guys did a great job. No one knew they would bring in the Warbirds or as many soldiers as they did, but you handled them pretty well."

"The boy helped us. We would have been doomed otherwise," Braden said.

"Well, maybe you should thank him."

A door opened on the left side of the room, and a boy with long blonde hair came in. Haley recognized him right away. It was the boy who was trying to tell her something in her dream.

The other kids didn't know who the boy was, but they all felt like they knew him. They just didn't know how.

"Hey guys." he said, in a much calmer voice than he had used before.

"Hello," the kids all answered.

"Good job out there. You all worked together and trusted each other like you were supposed to. I thought you weren't ready but you handled yourselves pretty well." The boy looked just a little older than Haley.

"Who are you?" Jack asked.

"You know who I am, don't you Jillian? You can feel it."

Jillian nodded. "Danny. But how?"

"It's a complicated story. The best way I can put it is that it was important for me to be here. I was needed."

"But you look older than me," Haley said.

"When you stay here full time, you grow up faster. I had to leave Earth so quickly because I needed to be trained right away."

"So you stay here all the time?" Braden asked.

"Yes. I am a teacher."

"Isn't Uncle Johnny a teacher?"

"Not exactly," Uncle Johnny answered.

"He's part time and I am full time."

"So, you'll never come back?" Jillian asked.

Danny shook his head. "No. But I sent someone else in my place. Take care of Timothy for me, okay?"

All the kids nodded. They knew Gabby's mother was going to have another baby.

"I can teach you guys all sorts of things. You haven't even started to learn your powers yet."

"Can you teach to me hold off Warbirds like you did?" Braden asked.

"Of course. And Jillian, I can teach you to create things you haven't even seen before. And we can make your strength even greater."

"Cool!"

"And Jack, imagine being able to send those bolts whenever and wherever you want."

"That would be great," Jack answered.

"And you," Danny said to Haley," I can teach you how to fly."

Chapter Fourteen

The kids talked with Danny for a bit, still amazed that it was actually him. The cousin they thought they had lost was with them, and they would get to know him. It seemed strange that he would be their teacher, but it also seemed right.

Danny went over to Gabby and picked her up. The sister he never got the chance to ever meet was in his arms and Haley thought she saw Danny cry but he quickly covered it up. Of all the things Danny had to give up by training full time, not getting to meet Gabby was the hardest. He kissed her on the forehead.

"Danny boy," Gabby said. "Hello."

"How did she know who you are?" Haley asked.

"I've talked to her in her sleep. I've been around her and her parents from the beginning. She must recognize my voice."

"That's amazing," Braden said.

"There will be a lot of amazing things to come," Uncle Johnny said, "but right now it's time to go home. You guys have had a rough day."

"You're telling us," Jack said.

Just then, the door opened again and an older man, who looked to be about 60 years old, came in the room. He had a long white beard and looked a lot like the statue they had seen.

"So here are our new Dream Fighters," the man said in a deep voice. "We have been waiting for a new class for some time."

"Yes," Uncle Johnny answered.

The man was tall, a few inches taller than Uncle Johnny, and very thin. He wore a cloak similar to Danny's, only his was white. It matched his beard.

"You did well today," he said. "I am Kal Ras, the leader of this academy. You can call me Kal. After you've trained with Danny for a while, I will teach you things you can't even dream of right now."

"That sounds great," Braden said.

"You all have your own special powers but you also have some powers in common. We will teach you to bring those out. But remember, the most important thing is that you tell no one in the real world about this. It is to be kept secret."

No one said anything but each of them wondered why it needed to be kept secret. Jack felt funny not being able to tell his parents. It almost felt like he would be lying.

"It's not like lying, Jack. It's the way it has always been done. Your mother was one of my students."

"She was?" Haley asked. "So we could talk to her about it?"

"She won't remember," Uncle Johnny answered. "Once Dream Fighters get to a certain age, they retire to start families of their own. When that happens, all their memories of what they did here are erased, for their own good. Your Mom and I fought some pretty cool battles back in the day."

"What about you?" Jillian asked.

"I think I might be leaving sometime soon, too," Uncle Johnny said.

"You're not leaving me to deal with Sarlak and the Gorgons," Danny said.

"You say you do all the work anyway."

"Well, you help sometimes." What Danny wanted to say was, if Uncle Johnny retired, he'd never be able to talk to him again. He would lose not only his teacher, but also his best friend.

"I'm not leaving yet, but soon, I think."

"Either way, we keep this a secret, even though many people in your family served with us. Your grandparents trained me," Kal said.

"Wow," the kids said together.

"Wow's a good word," Kal said. He looked to Uncle Johnny. "Get them home. We will start their training soon."

"When will we train?" Haley asked.

"At night, when you sleep," Danny said.

"Okay, let's go," Uncle Johnny said, and directed them to another door. They all walked through the door, and the next thing they knew, they were teleporting. Flashes of colors shined all around them and it felt like they were moving faster than they ever had before.

"When you wake up, only five minutes in the real world will have passed. No one in the house will have noticed anything."

"How is that possible?" Braden asked.

"We were in another dimension. It's like when you remember something. You can remember a whole day in just a few minutes, can't you?"

"I guess," Jack said.

"Well, it's like that. So, time passes differently in the two dimensions. Your training, which will take 6 hours in the dream world, will only be about 10 minutes of your sleep."

"That's a little confusing," Haley said.

"A lot of this stuff is going to be, but you'll start to get the hang of it as you learn."

"What about Gabby?" Braden asked. "How can we stop her from saying something?"

"You don't have to. Little kids say stuff all the time that parents don't pay attention to. You don't have to worry about that. We're just about there. Remember, don't say a word."

Haley woke up first. She felt dizzy, like she had been on a roller coaster. She looked and saw everyone wake up, even Uncle Johnny, who was sleeping in the recliner next to the couch.

"Okay," he said, "go back to playing your video game and I'll go back upstairs. Remember, don't say a word about what happened. Even to each other. Not when so many people are around."

They all nodded. Uncle Johnny went upstairs and Jack picked up the game controller. Somehow, after all they had done that day, video games didn't seem so exciting.

Chapter Fifteen

A week later, all the kids were at Jack's baseball game. It was a playoff game that his team had to win to go to the championships. With all of them there together, they felt the urge to talk about their training, which had started the night before. There were about to learn so many things at the academy. What they learned first was that Danny wasn't an easy teacher.

Jillian and Braden were sitting next to each other on the bleachers. Haley was standing by the fence. They were seated on the first base side, where Jack's team's bench was. Jack was stepping up to the plate.

The pitcher fired the first pitch. It was high and the umpire called it a ball. The third base coach shouted encouragement to Jack. There was a man on third in the bottom of the last inning. The game was tied, and there were two outs. It was all up to Jack.

"I wish there were an ice cream truck here," Jillian said. "I could really go for some right now."

"Ice cream," Gabby said.

Usually, there was an ice cream truck at the park. For some reason, there wasn't one this time.

The pitcher threw the next pitch and Jack swung. He fouled the ball toward the bleachers. Haley jumped, higher than she had ever jumped before, and caught the ball. It wasn't that high of a jump, but it was more than she would have expected.

"Nice leap," Braden said.

In the distance, the kids heard the sound of ice cream truck music. All the kids looked at Jillian and she shrugged.

"I didn't do anything," she said. "I think,"

Gabby looked at a man who was talking on his cell phone. He looked back.

"Listen Gina, I can't talk about this right now," he said into his phone, "There's a little girl here, and she's so cute I just have to get her an ice cream cone."

Haley, Jillian, and Braden looked at each other.

The pitcher threw another pitch and Jack hit it into the ground toward the second baseman. The runner on third hesitated and then started running toward home.

Jack took off toward first, but it looked like he would be out for sure. The second baseman bent down and picked up the ball. He threw it to first.

Right then, Jack's feet moved faster. He sped toward first base and beat the throw. He was moving faster than Haley had ever seen him run before.

"Oh boy," the kids all said together.

If they only knew what they would have to face next...

And now, a sneak peek at

The Dream Fighter Chronicles, Book Two:

Sarlak's Revenge

Haley stood on the edge of a high cliff. The wind blew through her hair. She took a deep breath, tasting the fresh air. She'd been to this spot before; it was where Danny had taught her to fly. She had to trust herself, he told her, and what better way to learn than by launching herself off a mountain? She was scared then, but now she had become comfortable with the place, coming here whenever she had some time away from training.

She stepped to the edge of the cliff, looking down at the valley below. There was nothing there but tan dirt and a tree or two. She turned her back to the valley, looked up at the clear blue sky, and fell backward. The same sensation she always felt when she did this came to her. First, a feeling of fear, of not being sure, and then the rush of excitement. She felt the air rush past her, and then she took control.

Out of the backward dive, she turned, and with the force of wind stronger than what was rushing toward her, she shot through the air, flying free. It was a feeling she had never felt before she learned to fly. It was better than she ever thought. It was perfect.

Haley floated for a little while, taking the time to enjoy the feeling of cutting through the air. It had taken a lot of time for Danny to help her perfect her ability to fly. He wasn't an easy teacher but she learned how to appreciate his methods and learn the way she needed to. She had complained to herself a few times about her training, but it all seemed worth it when she floated in the air the way she was.

She soared over the valley, noticing the birds flying below her, realizing she was doing something that everyone wished they could. She knew Danny and Uncle Johnny had told her not to brag about her powers, but it was hard not to enjoy them for what they were; special.

It was right when she thought about how special her powers were that she felt it. The feeling was both cold and angry at the same time. The anger was stronger, and she felt it overcome her. Something was terribly wrong, and she rotated to check if something was going on in the valley.

Far away, she saw her cousins locked in a battle, a battle very similar one to the one they fought against the Gorgons, back when Danny had saved them. She searched for him but couldn't sense him past the anger and fear.

With the sound of crackling thunder, she launched herself through the air toward the battle. She couldn't imagine why her cousins would fight without her, especially after they had been taught the importance of the group. She tried not to be upset. Something must have been really wrong for them to get involved without her.

As she rushed toward the battle, felt the heat of it, she noticed it moved further away from her. With an even louder cracking sound, she moved faster through the air, feeling the cold of it on her face.

The battle moved just as fast. The more she tried to get close to it, the more it stayed away from her. She was moving so fast at this point that her blonde hair was pulled straight back, and it felt like someone was pulling it out of her head.

That didn't matter to her. What mattered was why, if she was the leader of the group, the oldest, her cousins chose to fight a battle without her. Also, though she couldn't be sure, it seemed like they were losing it, and badly. They needed her.

She had learned a little about moving faster, of teleporting, but she wasn't that good at it because Kal didn't have the time to teach her. She wanted to learn, but most of the time, she worked with Danny on flying.

She tried to reach out to Danny in her mind. She also tried Uncle Johnny. She could sense one of them in the middle of the battle but she just couldn't tell which one it was.

Blasts of energy and light shot from the battlefield, and she got the sense that Braden was leading her cousins. She noticed his purple energy blasts attacking the enemy Gorgons, but it looked like the attacks weren't working. For every Gorgon he and her cousins fought off, three more appeared. And Haley could sense another presence. Actually, she sensed two.

One of the presences seemed familiar. The other, she recognized immediately. Before she had the chance to say something, she felt a power pulling at her.

Haley woke up, sweating. She thought she had been training but something didn't feel right. To be honest, she thought, something seemed very wrong.

Braden had been through this training before. He and Uncle Johnny had worked on it for weeks; he tried to concentrate his energy blasts, and Uncle Johnny clouded his mind his uncertain thoughts. The only difference was, this time the uncertainty was stronger than it ever had been.

Before him stood three Gorgons, the same way they appeared in the Simulation Room. Braden raised his right arm, balled it into a fist, and created a ball of purple energy in front of him. Then, as Danny taught him, he launched it toward the middle of where the three Gorgons stood.

Once there, he did what he was trained to do, he shot another burst of energy at the ball, causing it to explode and wipe out the Gorgons in its path.

The plan worked, like it always did, and the Gorgons disappeared in a flash of purple light. Even though it worked, something just didn't feel right. The whole time, Braden doubted it would work. He never felt that before.

Braden ran his hand through his brown hair and felt that it was wet. He was sweating, but why? He also felt scared, something he had been taught to control. If this was the Dream World, the one where he and his cousins had special powers, he shouldn't be sweating. He was only eight, but in the Dream World, he felt older, almost as old as he thought Haley felt, his cousin who was four years older.

Something was very wrong.

Immediately, the Simulation Room changed, and he was in the middle of a deep valley, one that looked like a desert. He felt a chill, and a strong fear, something he wasn't used to feeling.

When he looked to his left, he saw a huge battle going on, and he immediately felt the presence of his cousins. He didn't feel each one of them on their own, but he knew they all were there.

A strong blast of sound shocked him, and he wondered where it came from. None of them had learned a power like that, and the Gorgons only shot concentrated air as a weapon, so there must be someone new in the battle.

Braden was a little mad for not being told about the battle, but he tried to control his anger. Uncle Johnny had taught him to control his anger, even when he had to use his anger power.

When he was sure of which side his cousins were on, Braden created another ball of energy and launched it at the enemy. The ball rushed through the air but bounced off the target and came back toward him. It took all he had to avoid being hit by his own weapon.

Though he couldn't fly like Haley, Braden had learned how to raise himself off the ground. He did so, trying to get a better view of the battle. When he did, everything became blurry, like someone didn't want him to see it. He felt a great big fear, and he felt the need to run away.

He was taught to fight fear, but this one was harder than any other he ever felt before. He tried to get control of his mind back, but the more he tried, the more he lost it.

Before he had a chance to launch another energy ball, he found himself in his bed, and he was breathing heavy.

Braden didn't know if he was training that night, or just having a nightmare. All he knew was that he didn't want to feel that way again.

Gabby woke up from a bad dream. She didn't know what was going on, but she knew there was danger all around her. Only two years old, her idea of what was good and what was bad was clear. This was bad.

Even though she was a baby, Gabby had learned how to get out of her bed easily. She did so, and walked quietly to her parents' room.

There, she found her little brother's crib. Timothy was sleeping. She reached her hand into his crib and touched him on the forehead.

"Timothy ok," she said, "No one changing him."

Gabby went back to her room to sleep.

Jillian faced four Gorgons in the Simulation Room. Normally, she fought two Gorgons during training, but Danny was a tough teacher. She guessed he was trying to teach her something new. It wasn't the first time he did something like that.

Jillian treated this the same as every other training class. She rose herself off the ground, gathered her anger, and shot herself at the Gorgon in the middle. He was tall, over seven feet, and hairy, but she had learned a long time ago not to pay attention to that.

Before she reached the Gorgon, Jillian raised her fist, and then swung it right at her target. She had incredible strength, and she knocked the Gorgon out of the air. It disappeared.

The other Gorgons didn't react to the attack. Instead, they came at her. Jillian used the first power she ever learned and created a wall between her and them. Anything she thought about she could create.

"You need to see something," a woman's voice said in her head. "Your cousins are in danger."

All of a sudden, Jillian was taken to another place, this one a valley that looked like a desert. As soon as she got there, a cold feeling of fear took over her.

Jillian looked to the right, and saw a huge battle going on. She knew right away it was her cousins against the Gorgons. She wondered why they fought without her, but she realized they had no choice. She also felt they weren't all together. Someone was missing other than her.

She tried to move toward the battle, but she felt something stopping her.

"This isn't your battle to fight," the woman said in her head. She didn't know the voice, but she felt comfortable listening to it. She thought she should know who it was, but couldn't figure it out.

"I am supposed to watch," Jillian answered.

"Yes. And learn."

Jillian tried to watch the battle, but all she saw was energy blasts and huge bolts of electricity. The whole valley lit up in a huge display of light that looked brighter than a fireworks show on the Fourth of July.

Then, a huge explosion happened, and Jillian saw her cousins move away from the battle. She sensed who it was. It was Uncle Johnny and Danny coming to save them. She watched as the two of them fought off a huge Gorgon attack.

What happened next shocked her. A swirl of air, like a tornado, appeared, and a gigantic blast of energy came out of it. It looked like Uncle Johnny and Danny tried to defend themselves from it.

A dust cloud blocked her vision, and when it cleared, Jillian saw her cousins, and she saw Danny get up from the ground and dust himself off.

Jillian all of a sudden felt sad. She knew something she never, ever, wanted to know. The woman was trying to say something in her head but Jillian didn't listen. She also knew she was about to wake up in her room. What mattered most was the feeling she had.

Uncle Johnny was gone forever.

Made in the USA
Charleston, SC
04 January 2010